SILENCE FOR CARNIVORES
by: MAN BURMASTER

Immigrant Poon Press

SILENCE FOR CARNIVORES

CONTENTS:

"SPEAK! SPEAK!"

Yesterday I was giving an impromptu speech to The President at Best Buy. Yeah, in front of the flat screen televisions.

My friends, they say, "Huh?"

They say, "What you talkin 'bout? Dat funny, Carl!"

Then I say, "Huh?"

What so funny 'bout dat? It's true. I remember thinking, man I'm really gonna win big by telling Mr. President 'bout it. All about it, for sure. He's the President. Big men get it all. Big picture. Big men win big.

I started out by telling a story about my ex-girlfriend, Lily. It's that really funny story about how she almost caught her pantyhose on fire when she burnt the frozen Totino's pizza rolls in the toaster oven last year! Everybody loves Lily. Then I tell Mr. President about how she didn't burn herself, only her nude pantyhose, so it can be light-hearted and silly. She didn't get hurt. I got in a mood though, talking about Lily. Remembering Lily is like trying to contain a wildfire in a toaster oven. I told Mr. Prez about the nature of fire's burning. About how much irrelevance is caught of fire's consumption. Fire doesn't care what it burns, something as flimsy as pantyhose on a muscular womanly leg, or a pizza roll-it's the same to fire. It does its job.

It burns. We can only ever speak from the past. There's other ways to burn though, and other ways of speaking. There's an inverted burning that swallows all the petty crap in it's slow boozing. Even time, this fire can burn that away, too. A way of speaking that drinks up all hurts in its ever-loving, ever present, burn. Maybe that's what loving Lily has shown me.

I know that I'm going to win big. I win because I tell myself I do. I win because I have no stage fright, no honey in my heart anymore, and at this point it doesn't matter what I say.

I'm so charismatic it's crazy!

"Speak! Speak!"

The whole Secret Service are flippin' their lids over me.

"Speak! Speak!"

I'm suckin' all the air out of the room!

"Speak! Speak!" They all shout through the electronics and giant flat screen televisions. I see their faces on the screen but I know that they can't see me, at all. Their images are just on TV. They can't push or shove me away from Mr. President either. They have no clue what I'm saying. No clue about stupidity, winning big or just shooting the shit with the big man. They have no clue what's right in front of their faces. Who can say what it is to burn? They're there to serve and protect Big Men.

"Speak! Speak!"

…and I know that it doesn't matter what I said. They won't hear me any old way.

GOLDEN CANNONBALL OF SUCCESS.

A strange 'spiritual' creature is woman today, driven on and on by the evil demon of the old Logos, never for a moment allowed to escape and be herself. The evil Logos says she must be 'significant', she must, 'make something worthwhile' of her life. So on and on she goes, making something worthwhile, piling up the evil forms of our civilization higher and higher.

All women today have a large streak of the policewomen in them. Andromeda was chained to a rock and the dragon of the old form fumed at her. But poor modern Andromeda, she is forced to patrol the streets more or less in policewoman's uniform.

Ah God, Andromeda at least had her nakedness, and it was beautiful, and Perseus wanted to fight for her. But our modern policewomen have no nakedness, they have their uniforms.
And who would want to fight the dragon of the cold form, the poisonous old Logos, for the sake of a policewoman's uniform?

-DH Lawrence, Apocalypse

You golden cannonball of success! You've gotten everything that the lesser girls could only see on social media. What you want, you get. You don't have to wait nothing. You got it! With your skin stained the color of nicotine by so many sunny days on a private beach, you walk in and out of fancy hotels like it's your job. And it is.

The smooth arches of your freshly pedicured feet snuggly

in your killer heels, you walk. You walk like a self-reliant girl in high heels. I was impressed. We are all impressed. You are a modern woman, here at the Hotel Delano.

You're a success. You're a successful woman in this world. Just look at you. That's all we can do. When we look, we look in exclamation marks. Just look. At your body! At your pouty face! Look at your killer heels. At your outfit! This same outfit was in the latest issue of Vogue magazine! I even know how much it cost, plus tax.

We think in numbers instead of imagination. With a lack of imagination, it's easy to want to get to the punch line. With a lack of imagination, it's easy to talk in punch lines! To make the world flat, once again. And you sure do, you self-reliant success, you.

Men with beginnings and endings speak in beginnings and endings. Men who are directed, give you directions. It's an ever-easy line of logic to follow. Before and after follow each other. You have 5.7 M followers on Instagram!

Numbers are utilitarian. Shit, imagination is utilitarian. Memories are utilitarian. Only the useful is allowed to stick around. Logic is a lack of dreaming. A conclusion is all the compassion we are shown.

But that's alright when you're a success. You've made it. You have your own fashion line at Target. You know the fastest way to get somewhere: it's between two lines. You're vacation home looks like a modern alabaster palace where not even grass lives. Nobody lives here, except me.

In a weird twist of fate and luck, bad or good, you've let me stay here, in your home, where nothing living lives except a patch of giant, thorny roses at a forgotten corner of your property. To hang out here, without pay, because my payment is to live like your shadow. And eat like a shadow, too.

I don't wanna eat. I only wanna be left alone to walk your very secluded and vibrant rose garden at the edge of your property. To hear the earth rise in my ears and not give a fuck what you say about it. To feel nothing, air maybe, kneel against my insignificant, obscure heart. To let the silence that's everywhere, in the high, and in the low spots, be all the friendship and generosity I need. To imagine. To daydream. It's good to be left alone, in your high-thread count sheets, without a crummy past to run from, to not think about injustices or commonplace philosophies that make a sick war where golden cannonballs of success are murderously hurled across a perfectly peaceful blue slice of sky. And the successful women say, yeah. I have drive. Then the magazine's report, yeah. They have drive! I don't want to continue that.

It stinks. She texts me a thousand times with the words CALL ME.

Do you think I wanna call this girl?

Not really. I drink a glass of wine in two minutes and call her. I'm feeling warm and fuzzy as she quickly talks. Holy really. I feel so goddamn holy that who knows what she's really saying but whatever she's saying she means it! I try not to get too nervy about all the meaning and purpose she's throwing around.

There's a pause. I listen to the silence. Silence doesn't throw around stupid shit like meaning and purpose. Silence is everybody's friend. She breaks the silence and politely asks me to pick her tarot card for the day.

She likes me to do this for her. I walk back inside where I have left the door open and now there's an ugly brown bird flying around the spacious white kitchen. I ignore the bird flapping about and begin the long walk back to my room. I carefully walk across the slick, polished white marble floor and stare blankly through the floor to ceiling glass windows that surround the corridor, to get my tarot cards. Nothing moves outside.

Outside of my room, there's a dead brown bunny on the white marble floor. I can't help but to cry. The bunny was foaming at the mouth before she died. Thick coagulated spittle surrounds her delicate mouth, a mouth without sharp teeth. Her eyes and face are also triple the size of its cute furry body.

I know the bunny ate poison that the gardeners just put out. She doesn't know about the bunny. She doesn't care about the poison that makes her roses so strong, colorful and giant. She doesn't know I am crying and she doesn't know that I'm afraid to close the door, ever, and so who really knows what wildlife lives in her white palace?

She's talking again, very quickly. Now she tells me the guy that I'm seeing is cute but ultimately worthless so have fun while it lasts. I reach my room and get the cards.

I shuffle for a while she talks about her life. Twenty minutes go by and she's still talking. I'm still shuffling. She finally ends.

It is number 13, The Death card. I begin to tell her about new beginnings and the possibility, every day, for new life, but she says that's unfortunate and that I probably picked that because I was in a bad mood about my new boyfriend. That's not her card.

Click. She has hung up. I close my eyes as I pass the dead bunny and walk toward the kitchen. When I get there, I pour another glass of wine.

The brown bird maniacally flits around the ceiling. Its flying is panicked. Her flight is so scared and fast that it looks like a little brown shovel digging, just digging the air. Just digging on nothing. Digging with feathers rather than steel. Just digging for what?

Before credit cards and dollar bills, anything valuable was buried. Pearls come from cold deep water. Diamonds and jewels from deep, filthy pits. Gold from dank, hidden earth. The bird kept digging at the immensity of silence.

All the bullshit of life, all the diamonds in the rough, so to say, live in anonymous places. But who cares about a dirty diamond when you can just buy them with your success and motivation and drive, without blood or dirt, like the diamonds at Harry Winston on Rodeo Drive?

You think it's real, this sort of going up. Nobody questions the easy logic. Up is a direction you can sense. What's there to see? The successful girls are pretty in an adrenaline-mad shopping rush. The failures have their own adrenaline mad shopping rushes.

Listen, I don't wanna talk inside my head. I don't wanna talk inside my head in monochromatic tones and provisionally eat snacks that come from factories and talk about the things that I see on TV with my girlfriends or employer. I don't wanna bitch when life gives me what I don't want, and I don't wanna act smug and aloof when life gives me what I do want. I want a place away from above and below, a place where I don't need to be entertained by this or that.

The small bird with the big black eyes that never blinks, digs forever not realizing the door out isn't always up. I drink some more. I admire this nameless bird.

But, you!

You are a success.

A golden cannonball of success. But wait, she's calling me, again.

FLORIDA, NEVER.

Great Mamma D. chose to think that I was just going schizoid like everybody else in my family when I told her it was high time for me to quit work, buckle down on my high school studies, and prep for Harvard. Mamma D. believed in me but didn't believe my high-flautin Harvard stories.

There's two things about my lineage. We're all from Palm Coast, Northern Florida. That's the first thing. In Palm Coast, there ain't no 'high times'. We live in a swamp. All bound to sink. Then, the other thing is nobody never leaves Palm Coast, Northern Florida.

There's something else about my family, something that you can't number or measure like you can say who's first place or second place. Something you can't tell a story about, or educate, or rationalize. It has no genesis like that. Something of a great mystery, the way all mysteries can't help but to be great.

We're all nuts. In my family, we go nuts right here under the low humid sky in Palm Coast, Northern Florida. What's going on is that when you're nuts, you can go everywhere without actually leaving your home. When you're nuts, you only think you're traveling to big fancy places or if you prefer, big skanky places. Really, though we go nowhere. Really.

Uncle and Great Mamma D. are sensitive to these things. Uncle and Great Mamma D. look alike. They both have primordial bodies that seem made of sandbags instead of muscle and bone. Bodies so strong and big they didn't have no need for anything so hard or smart like bones or a head. With bodies ready for disaster, Mamma D. and Uncle ain't wantin' to hear nothin' about Harvard!

Uncle says that going nuts is like travelling blindly through a steakhouse's kitchen. I didn't know what that meant. I asked him to just explain himself. He shook his head like something wrong with me. Then he digs his heel in the gravel and rubbed it around, made that gritty, moanin' sound with the sharp rocks rubbing against the hard earth like he so wise that the earth done do his talkin' now.

To me it didn't matter if you were blind or not, damn near everybody knows what steak on a bbq smells like! Smells good!

"Is it like smelling a fine feast fit for emperors but not knowing where it come from?" I said stupidly. He rubs his foot in the gravel some more.

"Or even, what such delicious food looked like?"

He calmly tells me not to wax poetic like I was inclined to do. Just to shush.

So I did. We sat in silence looking from the porch. It was a breezeless day. Gnats danced under mad clumps of Spanish moss on the sinewy Pecan tree I've known since I've been a baby. The heavy Bermuda grass was still wet from last night's rain, the humid sound of cicadas in the pine across the dirt road. Mosquitos biting our already bitten legs.

Then he says, "Child you do not understand. It's like drowning, Huddie." Huddie is my name.

"Drowning or waking from a very nice dream and under-standing just about everything so joyously in your heart, that you can't help but to know that you've been living all wrong. Yesterday is wrong. Tomorrow sure to be wrong, too. You can't help but be grateful for drowning, dyin' quick like that. So, yeah, Huddie, it's like drowning. Smelling something delicious from meat that you cannot really see before you drown."

Now the other girls at school call me all sorts of things. Psycho. Strange. Violent. Possessed. Oh, it's the stuff for dead French poets and not for a poor black girl from Palm Coast, Florida but when you're crazy what does geography matter, huh? I didn't mind the names but I did mind the way everyone would push on me and push. Calling me and my family all sorts of ugly names. Wanting me to push back, knock in their teeth and ribs in like rotten walls of a long-forgotten basement. But I couldn't be petty like them. I'm not foolish. Crazy girls are a great many things but they ain't petty.

Experience and knowledge are brothers. For the poor crazy bastards, experience first, then you get to know about it. For the lucky ones' knowledge first, then they can see it in another person. Like they got it all figured out. Like they satisfied with words and stones and not with bread and water and wine. Still, it's just a way to order things. Don't each person got their own particular way of smirkin' at you. They smirk at you through what they've come to experience. Smirk at you through the things that they know.

Smirkin' is smirkin'. Smirkin to prove our cruel but collective sense of reality that poises some as crazy, or poor, and others as evolved, or rich.

Great Mamma D. don't have to smirk nothin'! How Mamma D. laughed from the pit of her stomach when I told her I was going to Harvard! She just laugh and laugh and laugh like I'm some clown come to entertain her for 'while.

This went on for a while. Then Mamma D. met a psychic. Just randomly, you know, probably in the aisle at The Food Lion. Well, a week later they had an appointment at the psychic's house. The psychic poured Mamma D. tea even though Mamma D. would never drink hot tea on her own, on a hot ass day, no less, but didn't Mamma D. drink it down as she didn't wanna offend this gifted, high priestess. This psychic told her that I was going to affect many people, so many, and my name would be known in writing.

"Me a writer from Harvard?!" I said to Great Mamma D.'s face when she done came back. She said I'd have lots to say, lots to tell about, and millions of dollars, just millions! It was then at the psychic's house, with a hot, sweaty face and swollen neck from too much hot tea, that Great Mamma D. believed and encouraged me, as best as she knew how. Maybe I'm not headed to the Looney Bin, Northern Florida after all. Maybe I'm not so Looney Tunes.

Harvard?! Maybe the curse of my lineage has been lifted in me. What a blessing supreme to consider it just once. Mamma D. even says that I don't have to work so many hours at Victoria's Secret at the Town Valley Mall so I can study more for my exams. I only work there part-time.

Harvard undergraduate, huh? I slowly tapped my finger between my lips considering it. I say it again in my mind's eye. But I can't see Harvard at all. I only feel how much I love my family. And then, immediately, I knew if I ever do go to Harvard, I'll never really leave Florida. Never.

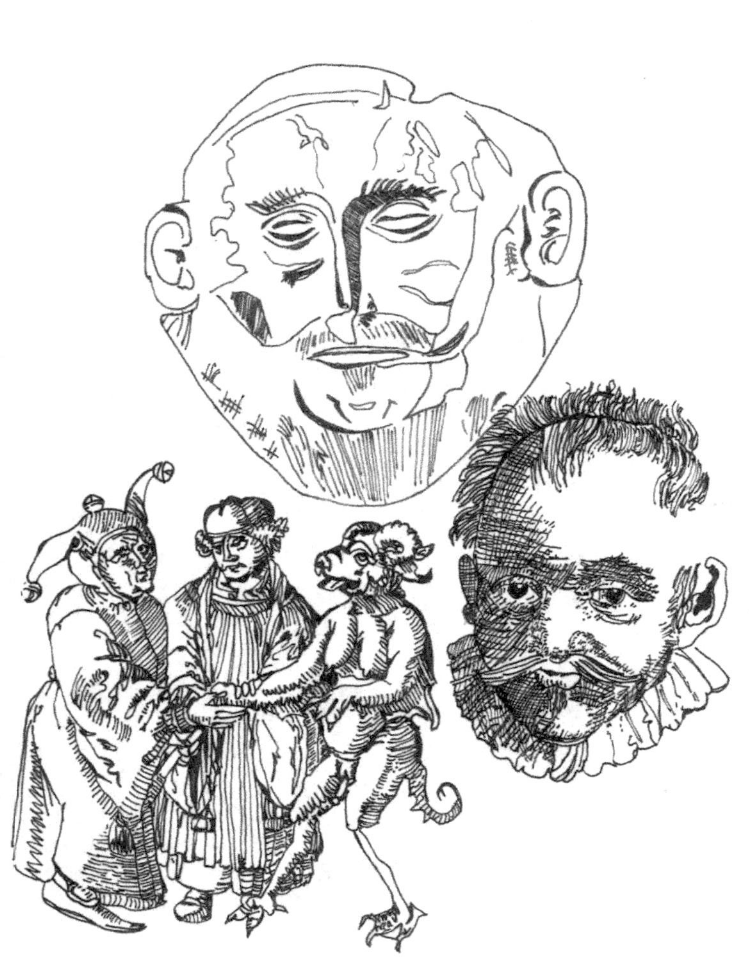

MIKES.

The housewives aren't interested in perverts unless it's on prime-time television. That's what I've learned from both the TV and the housewives talk in my town. Tonight, the anchorman reports that Mike has been arrested for internet pedophilia. Good thing I got a new plasma TV screen last week so I don't miss out on any syndicated neighborhood dysfunction. The anchorman's face is at least two feet tall and one foot wide. As the sound of the anchorman's monotone narration rolls over Mike's hidden and heinous sexual life, I'm impressed at the smoothness of the anchorman's tan. My God, did he just get back from Miami? He looks so sun kissed. His tan face is so smooth, without wrinkle or blemish. His face is a mask of orange flesh that his thick blonde eyebrows crack, the way orange heat cracks sidewalks and old roads. It's weird, you know, watching a man with tan makeup talk to camera about the sexual sins of a man nobody ever paid attention to except for now, except through his sexual deviance, a man like Mike.

The pedophile, Mike, walks with a paper bag over his head, nearly six centimeters tall. He walks digitally, flatly, across my new TV screen. Two obese cops in the standard black uniform lead him down the white courthouse stairs.

"Mike Douglass was a factory worker at the Red Wing Shoe plant in Red Wing, Minnesota." The news man booms. Hey, wait. I work there, too. Do I know the pervert?

Huh. Mutants in makeup mime The Corporation's news, Mikes keep on being Mike and the housewives, you know they're everywhere now, monitoring everything, I guess, keep the world turning. I take another big hit of my spliff. I smoke the good shit through the workweek. It makes my time sweeter. I blow the smoke around the image of Mike with the bag over his head, handcuffed, and lead into the back of a police car by two uninvolved looking police. With his new label as pedophile, this is the most attention that Mike has ever received in his whole lonely, perverted life.

"Mike Douglass held the Guinness Book of World Records, 1997-2009 for the most baseball hats collected." Is announced as each room of Mike's mother's house is spanned, showing the hat collection on every wall. Mike's mother is a decrepit woman in a pastel pink and white moo moo with large blue flamingos flying nowhere. Just stuck on the old rag that covers her skeleton.

She shakes her head. Then she throws a bony, wrinkled arm at one full wall of his world of baseball hats. A clip shows Mike with one of his beloved baseball hats on.

I see that face. I know that face!

"Is that!" I yell.

"No!"

"It couldn't be!"

Nobody answers me. Besides the bright flat screen TV, my living room is cheap brown, full of brown smells, odd dents in cheap walls, dust and dead insects looking for somewhere better to be before they died and buried their tiny bodies in the dirty mauve carpet. Ashtrays, things never dead, never alive, broken things surround me.

"I know.....Mike! We work at the shoe plant together. He's a man of great work ethic and caliber. A man who never caused anyone any wrong." I say from my worn brown recliner, to nobody.

Another news story comes on. Mikes prime time is over.

"Mike Douglass! You son of a bitch!" I shake my head and look for my stash to roll another joint. The pigsty around me says shit.

Was he a pedophile? There's no response. The silence of my dingy brown living room. They were damn right about his hat collections. He was obsessed with it. Mike would go on and on about how baseball caps were the modern version of a Greek death mask. Well, we didn't know what he was talking about. He spoke in riddles. Something about ripping the face off of identity, I dunno! He sounded like a mouse who spoke in Grateful Dead lyrics. Listen, I like a couple of Grateful Dead songs, don't get me wrong. I know we all have a skeleton underneath our flesh that will outlast any circumstance or lotto we may win, or face that we might have. We didn't know why the Greeks had death masks. Or what the death mask was. Mike said it was a memento of the dead.

Maybe like a skeleton. Skeletons, we all have one. It was a weird thought to think about my skeleton, the same bones that held me up in my recliner, outlasting even the notion of 'me'. I rummaged around a small wooden drawer. Playing cards, ashes, dust, papers, old pens, rubber bands, old gum, paper clips, dirty screws, old plastic wrappers, a mini-tennis ball, old remotes and batteries. Where is it?

I get out of my recliner which is a big deal. I moan and groan. I carefully position and hoist myself out of the nest. I shuffle through the brown noise of the brown smells of my cheap brown living room toward the freezer. In an old Breyer's strawberry ice cream tub, I knew I had a hidden stash. I open it. I smooth out the crinkles in the baggie before I open it. I roll a joint and smoke it with the freezer open. Yes, yes- I whisper back, nodding to the freezing cold air, my pal cold air. I hold the smoke in as long as I can. I blow out congealed yellow smoke that looks like exotic seaweed for faeries.

Mike had a neurological condition that rendered his IQ to the level of a functional 2nd graders IQ. We all knew that. He wasn't all there. Did the news and police know that? Did they care? Now I know I'm fucked up enough. I get fucked up and ask myself who cares about what. And I'm swimming in it. The back and forth of questions and answers. I'm pretty sure in this consensus reality of news reports, the makeup of tan mimes, criminals and police to man the fort, that good behavior is only a deviant of bad behavior.

There's so much bad behavior on the news. They'd make you think that we were just loaded skinsacks of bad behavior. Cooped up in factories in the daylight, we willingly sit in smelly barrooms in a moonlight that's too high up for us to ever see. We live away from grass fields and housewives with our TVs. We'll only get on TV if we act up, so we do. At least we can try. I try not to get too pooped over it. I smoke. I smoke and take long walks around the town at dusk, after working at the shoe factory and before the bar. I walk but hardly walk, as if I was shuffling up against something impossible like a cold, icy mountain.

It's the end of the summer. I like to stand at the edge of the community soccer fields and look as far as I can into the distance with the shouts, cheers, laughs and screams of a late Thursday afternoon. Let it all splash over me. The competitive sounds of kids, kids playing sports and the pushed sounds work their merry way through my crazy thoughts. I stand tall.

The sun is going down in a red and pink haze. Families shout at their brothers or sons on the field and it makes me feel okay. More than okay, safe. They belong to one another. Life hasn't broken them. The new mothers share disaster stories they heard on the news to the old mothers, and the old mothers share disaster stories back. They talk in news headlines and frowns. One mother looks up and over at her son. A quick smile. Arms wave. Hello, Goodbye.

The son ignores her, his face is shaded by a baseball hat. Nobody can erase what already exists. Fluffy clouds from the rain we had are carnation pink, melon and plum in the humidity. I stare out and out until my stare blurs into a kaleidoscope of reds with the safe sports sounds around me. Every color of red is working its way from the soccer field like a really badass Russian ballet where every blade of grass is a fucking pro prima ballerina. Seeing the grass brushed red and dancing like it is, I know that the earth is a big boot factory where we all work. The anchorman, me, the housewives, the kid baseball players, all the Mikes, we're all just doing our jobs at the mysterious boot factory.

Soon there's boots everywhere, like a boot factory worker's dreamscape. Sea glass green boots against cherry boots until the grass is unsettled, and boots engulf this small town. I imagine it.

I imagine it all. That's all I got. What lives within. Then the clutter of boots from this small town with its safe jeweled colors moves towards the big city. Then after it's infected the city with its bright red dance it moves up and over the land toward the silence, brine and awe of the ocean. The wet color of bittersweet boots, I say, and it sounds right. The pert color of salmon boots, overgrown and ratty boots, all over the ocean. Far away from here, so deep, so lovely, an ocean where no human can ever step one real boot on.

But at the soccer field it smells crisp and earthly, like healthy grass freshly cut with the occasional waft of over-active adolescent sweat glands. Ek, it's putrid really. Bones are the only house for eternity. The grass is the only enduring flower for the dead. It doesn't matter if you get caught up in hats, makeup or the news or boots. It's the normal people of the world who really enjoy hearing about the abnormal. The functional who put the grossly dysfunctional on their news channels. The starved imagination that makes for logic. It's every day stuff.

Thirsty and hungry and sleepy and desiring and logical currently…. I search…. Yes…. I search for…something…the colors have died out. The game is over. Everybody is gone.

All the shouts, cheers and laughs have disappeared. My dream of boots is gone too, leaving me sad. It's quiet. The wind against the steel poles are the only thing left that keeps screaming. I lean back into the cold steel pole of the field's lights. I put my ear against it just the same. My cheek is hot, but the pole is turning cold. The sun is dying at 8:30 at night and the temperature has dropped. The small yellow bugs fly around the light that looms overhead. I get comfortable as I search the flat land to the horizon until everything near is blurred like its far away and outta reach. There's no reds left.

It's too dark for red. I shall no longer pretend to care. I know I'm really one of those bugs in a swarm, waiting frantically for the dying sun. Talking to myself about boots, brown heat, skeletons and pink housewives' frowns.

I feel the heat of summer under my skin in the dark.

The house of baseball hats is empty. Hats nobody would choose to wear.

Is that!

No! I can't believe it.

Mikes.

He found virtues and reason equally critical and lonely. But he would never actually go out and say that. We all have our ways of living inside the hard walls of our stories, our factories, hats and grasses. We all have our own boots to crush it all away.

I imagine things I don't see on prime time. I imagine boots crushing anything so unfair, so strong as to survive. All probably contributed to his obsession for collecting baseball hats.

AMERICAN 'CINEMA' FOR DOSTOEVSKY.

Goodness is one thing with me and another thing to a Chinaman, so it's a relative thing.

Or is it?

Or isn't it? Is it not relative?

A treacherous question, you laugh. You won't laugh if I tell you it's kept me awake two nights! I wonder how people can live and think nothing about it. Vanity!

-Dostoevsky, The Brothers Karamazov

Cinema is different from a movie and I learned this from my ex-boyfriend who went to college. Cinema is highbrow and a movie is lowbrow. He explains. I know that we're all performers, performing in some performance, to be broad about it all but you can't say it like that to him cuz he gets upset about being broad. Being broad is generalizing and generalizing is only a respectable form of bigotry, to him. He explains, again. That's what he taught me reality was really, The Masquerade. Everybody wears a character or personality, like a mask, to survive in The Masquerade. Some are born with better masks than others. Some are crafty and make better masks. There's no individuality. No justice or equality or freedom in this reality even though The Masquerade carks about these nice words all the time. It's all part of the show. You get what you pay for. People who pay for things wanna know that they got the most bang for their buck.

I'm participating in my own bad movie. That's how I handle myself: this is a bad movie and I, I, with the given name of Karen S. Benton, am only a hologram of light on the big screen. The just and the villains have equally clean manicured hands without blemish on their great faces.

In the masquerade you could say, 'hey, look, there's a celebrity playing a bum 'outside' in the 'snow!' But it's all contained in a soundstage that is a comfortable 70 degrees. Nobody is hurt that way. There's no outside. A celebrity is acting like a normal, regular man making a snowman! How cute. Let's give him a million dollars! And later on, as you walk out of the soundstage, and outside where your car's parked, somewhere on Wilshire in 90-degree dry Los Angeles heat, make sure to tip your hat to the real bum.

Or piss on him. That's what Dostoevsky mentioned in the book, The Brothers Karamazov. Mainly, of all the dumbshit my exboyfriend taught me, I actually liked reading Dostoevsky. Dostoevsky said go take a piss on the real bum, because you do that, anyways! My exboyfriend didn't have to provoke me to read books like these. Of course, I wanted to read books like these. What a stand-up guy to point that out, huh? I mean geez!

All this performing, I don't know, it's been going on since Dostoevsky was alive, for crying out loud. You take something that's real and most obvious-something that's painful, painful because it cracks you up inside. Then spruce it up, spruce up the pain, until it's hollow, pretty enough, and inhumanly crude but nobody notices cuz its inside of you. You carry it around with you. But it's too heavy. You can't pretend anymore. You're all ripped apart. That's a movie for you. In movies, it's a question of distance, darkness and bad role-playing my ex-boyfriend lectured me.

I'm frightfully shy and feel ill-equipped for regular life. I try to survive, I guess even though I know that not surviving is better. So far, this distance/darkness/bad role-playing thing is what has made me both an uncaught pickpocketer and tolerant of terrible things that frighten me, sometimes. Pickpocketing is about how close you can get to somebody without them ever sensing your hands. It's like the Kantian concept of a noumenon, which I also learned from a different ex-boyfriend, who also went to a fancy college in New

England.

I try not to ask too many questions. I didn't want him to think that I was stupid or nothing. I do remember that I timidly asked my boyfriend at the time, 'Is Noumenon like God?'

He replied, 'No! No, Karen!' Like he was disgusted. He paused while my cheeks burned from embarrassment and stared at me for a while. 'No,' he replied with acid civility and cringed at the clean floor around us while I told myself not to cry.

Then he told the floor, 'it's a waste of time to try to verbalize it!'

It's about knowing about things without the senses to guide you. Knowing without having a thought about it. It sounds like pickpocketing to me. And if you're good, they won't even feel you. Still, I wonder when we'll give up on trying to define ourselves or others. I mean, who cares? When are we going to stop stirring shit and trash in the same cardboard character's skulls and then give face that holds the skull a million dollars?

When am I going to see anything new at the movies? When are we going to forget about the trash and sail toward clear, sunny skies with very pretty sails that make heroic sounds, like real canvas sails, as they slice through the air while the boat's belly echoes off of deep blue water? I wouldn't live in a movie then. I wouldn't live in The Masquerade. I'd live in the middle of the ocean. It'd be nice if I wasn't so poor. Then, I'd really sail!

But I say, Karen?! Honestly. Really, Karen. Then what?!

Well, then what? You wanna million buckeroos, Karen?! I scoff at myself.

I'm not defined by my circumstances good or muddy. I don't know nothing about the future. So who cares if I'm poor, been born poor and all I've known is poor? Why escape it? To move into a prettier costume with a prettier house that I hafta actually pay for, that I am obligated by law to pay for every month and that way, hafta, hafta stay in? What will that do?

Nothing. I say quietly to myself. Nothing. Just nothing. Make me a better doll for The Masquerade. I understand that this is still just another movie. Same production company. Me. The World. The Erudite. The ExBoyfriends. I'm only in a rotten movie, Karen S. Benton. I'm only a hologram of light on the big screen of lights. It's fucking nothing. If I perform anything, it begins with this light. This frail, perishable screen of lights. If I break my own heart, more light, I'm just opening up for more light. If I rip anything, it starts with this light. I just don't wanna go on and on about it. It's nothing, really. And nothing belongs to me here. Nothing. Not even my ideas, not even my name, not my sadness, everything belongs to The Masquerade.

BUNNI.

The hair on my cousin Bunni LaGuarda Leon's face grew in long, thin strands. Soon, it was all over her face. On her forehead, nose, under her eyes, everywhere. The hair was the texture of a pretty white lady's hair and the color was gold. The flimsy broken color gold, like splintered gold-leaf used to globe in the holy's heads in Renaissance paintings. The gold hair enveloped Bunni's face until she looked like she had a snarled golden beehive on her head. It literally grew overnight on her caramel skin. Don't worry, she could breathe just fine.

It was a noteworthy color of gold, though. Even now, I can't stop thinking about it. That's why I mention it the way I do. I thought the gold hair was beautiful. Really, a transcendental experience, seeing beauty like that. Beautiful in an unconventional, terrifying and imposing way--the way real beauty tends to be really frightening, so out of the ordinary, if you consider it. We are of Mexican-American descent, and nobody in our lineage has ever possessed a strand of flaxen hair.

Where did it come from? Why did it happen to Bunni? Bunni had long black hair and black hair on her arms, normal black hair, nothing hairy or abnormal but black, and a small pretty face with black doe eyes. Her eyes were so round and black they seemed wet all the time like she had tears covering them. She sorta looks like the Virgin Mary, as most of the women in our family do. After a week of feeling ridiculous with the gold beehive of hair on her face, Bunni grew impatient. She took a cheap pink BIC razor to the knotted gold, her unbelievable Aryan nest, on her face. She shaved well, looked pleased at the reflection of her face in the mirror, and then slept.

It grew back overnight. Now, it grew thicker. The golden hair surrounding her face turned so thick it was biblical, really. It looked like incomprehensible and senseless revenge from a wrathful Old Testament God. The golden hair was beautiful beyond beauty, to me. It wouldn't be ignored. It existed and didn't force itself to conform. Who is blessed so much that you are given such an extraordinary, individualized curse of hair, blonde hair like a wedding veil? I began to look at Bunni differently. Not because of the hair but because the blessing that the hair signified. The hair grew stronger when you tried to get rid of it. It did not procrastinate. It knew of life, of being alive. It knew what it was there for. It knew how to be creative and receptive. There's an immediacy to this, huh? I respected this beauty. I am a woman, too.

Now the hair looked like a straw field full of sunshine, hunched peasants with thick one-of-a-kind outfits, and silence. It seemed eerie. Like a straw field that VanGogh would hang out in, walk and paint and cry and hopefully laugh in. Like the kind of open silent, gold earth that you wouldn't mind dying in. Maybe killing yourself in, like Van Gogh. I couldn't help but to cry around her beehive of hair, really, my heart felt so gigantic and raw.

The hair became a work of art. Bunni spent many humid summer days in south Queens, inside the air-conditioned nail salon on the first floor of her apartment building waxing. Then, when that failed, she lasered. And when that failed, bleaching the hair. Our cousin said bleach would weaken the hair and eventually, make the hair snap off.

Bunni stopped going outside at all. She sat in an office chair, her body sunken and dejected in her tight magenta tang top that said Angel, in cursive, with a halo over the A and even tighter white jean shorts where the skin of her back would fold over her waistband.

I would go with her just to make sure she was alright. In the period of an hour, she pulled her shirt down in the back, to cover her neon yellow thong that came out of her shorts, no less than ten trillion times. She was self-conscious and embarrassed about the extra weight she had gained from not going outside. Not going anywhere, only sitting in front of the TV, hiding. Feeling like she was dying and a freak for her work of mysterious art. It was painful to see her so embarrassed about something so exclusive, alive and resilient.

Months went by and she kept bleaching the growing strands of hair on her face but they kept growing. By winter it got so bad that her neck and ears were albino and cracked like an elephant's pachyderm from all the bleaching. She cried a lot. I hated to hear it. It made me panic to hear her cry. It was like when we were little girls, holding each other and crying in closets while the adults fought drunkenly with each other. The sound of manly insults. Furniture moving. Glass shattering. Women screaming. There was nothing I could do. We took up praying to La Milagrosa, like we did when we were little girls.

La Milagrosa is the most powerful and benevolent holy woman around and everybody on Bunni's Hispanic block in Queens knows this. Petitioning for intercession to La Milagrosa is a no-brainer in non-medical but life-threatening cases. We sent a mass email to all the women we knew we were related to, and about fifteen of our cousins and aunts began a woman's circle on Thursday nights. After work, I traveled all the way from the West Village to Queens serried against hundreds of other exhausted business professionals, for Bunni's recovery. In our abuelita's narrow, humid living room that smells like fresh tortillas, tomatoes and fried cheese without fail, we light religious candles with holy cartoons on their labels praying for Bunni, praying for La Milagrosa to intercede, because we didn't know what else to do. Bunni doesn't ever leave our abuelita now. Anyways, nobody told Bunni that growing hair on her face like that was a symptom of 5-DhW. How could we know? It was all so new back then.

5-DhW is a virus that only affects people who are prone to compartmentalizing their emotions/thoughts into pre-existing, consensus-tried storylines. Finding these storylines is cake. They show up in every major media outlet such as magazines, motion pictures, TV popular blogs, and books. All you have to do is insert the selected storyline into your life. With the magic realism of identification, and more specifically, with the psychological content that comes from feeling abused, married to the sociological Procrustean Bed inherent in the narrative-well, it's easy to infect the masses.

Everybody becomes the same. When mass amounts of people are really the same they are easy to dominate. 5-DhW isn't deadly but it makes you angry, hairy and confused. It makes your womanly life every woman's life. It makes your manly life every man's life. People get excited about this, about sharing stories, more drama and 'relating'. These people have no sense of horror or history. They only have their assumptions about 'life'. The women who are excited are also the women who are also envious and cranky. The men who are excited are also the men who are competitive and aggressive. But what can be done?

For Bunni? If Bunni left Queens, all she ever knew, our abuelita, and all her family, moved to Bali for a month and fervently prayed to La Milagrosa, or got rid of Milagrosa and just meditated, while eating organic, foreign vegetables and fruits and drinking fresh mountain spring water, the same pH as her own blood, then found her soul mate and wrote a NY Times best-selling book and sold the rights of her storyline to become a Hollywood blockbuster, she still wouldn't be cured. That story was already had. That's how 5-DhW works. The cure was to be something brand new. The golden hair that choked her face would fall out if she dived deep into the unknown. That's it. And there, in some land completely bizarre and strange, completely mundane and familiar-- it'd be like paradise. But, what does a girl named Bunni from Queens know about Paradise, or strange, and furthermore, where to find such a place?

Overnight she was cured and why?

My other friend, Bunni, is an art dealer in the West Village.

He has a proclivity towards paintings by trust fund kids from New England with hot shit art school degrees. The paintings look like cute shit that's all over Etsy now but Bunni tells me I don't understand contemporary post-internet art so well with such cretin opinions. He also sells paintings by celebrities, harlot/bad-girl inspired paintings and paintings by motorcycle rebels from the USA in the 1960s.

I work under him. Basically, doing his bitch work. He's nice enough to employ me but he sorta has to be nice, so it's really not that nice. We've known each other since childhood and I'm basically like his sister. We've never been apart.

We grew up staunchly Catholic in a tiny West Texas town and now we both live in Manhattan, so I understand him well. Bunni has blonde hair, blue eyes and an athletic body. When he was younger he was a Ralph Lauren model and that was exciting for our small town. Now, he drinks heavily and likes male Asian prostitutes that look, in some way, much like Carravaggio's rendition of Bacchus. These nervous, international men with pretty faces that he sleeps with are more chatty and exotic than our past, our shared desperate past, in West Texas. It's nice to look at another's face and think of a modern version of a Carravaggio and listen to them tell another great story about their great life or great fashion they wear than deal with your scummy past, or consider why you're such a prick to everybody, or even, if an invented, self-made heaven is really the typical hell?

When he drinks he insults whoever is around and if he drinks enough, he insults the people who are no longer around. That's how I know when he's really toast. He starts insulting all the clowns we knew in West Texas. Since he makes six figure deals, on the daily, has a PhD from Columbia, and slanders everybody with original, sometimes ingenious slurs like he's some aristocratic cowhand, people think he's really grand. Just a genius! They like that clever machoism in New York City.

Well, I knew him before these things. He knows not what

he does. He doesn't know any better than to believe in his hell so much he thinks it's heaven. His hell is the typical hell that everybody else calls heaven. It's part of the 5-DhW virus. When you win big, you are permitted to call hell, heaven. That way you can transmit the virus to other bodies while keeping your own sick confusion inside.

If he really thought of his life the way it is, he wouldn't be able to handle it. I just know it. He'd jump into the East River and wouldn't even worry about getting dirty or diseased. He'd be that upset. And we don't like germs or untidiness, in general.

Regardless of what you think about Thomas Kinkade, he really is the American Carravaggio, an exceptional American Bunni Rabbit, and as such, is a master of American chiaroscuro. Kinkade knows what color our collective shadows are. They're pink. Pink and a flimsy white- white, white, white. When you wear light colors, nobody gets too bummed out feels the rage of manmade injustice or gets grimly philosophical. It pisses serious academic people off, of course that our shadows are pink and white. They want to be all Parisian and have black, seedy shadows and Art Nouveau black cats with eyes the color of evil Leprechauns and wear black cashmere turtlenecks while drinking Chartreuse outta real, fimbriated crystal glasses. They want to wonder if they're alive or not. But you can't spend your life listening to some bunk jazz in cafés! Come on, get real. They won't. They'll never leave New York City or Paris or wherever means money now. You bet they'll at least try to listen to bunk jazz for a lifetime.

Away from civilization, back in West Texas, my Dad, Bunni, knows about the color of our American shadows. Bunni saw Eat, Pray, Love and now wishes light and love to each thing he comes to think about, but he won't tell nobody else that because they'd call him a pussy, for sure. So he tells me.

He doesn't give a damn if they do! He tells me that, too. He'll wish er'y damned thing light and love if he damned well pleases. He says. When I talk to him, once a week on

Sundays, as planned, he says life's so damned good that it's like livin' in a Thomas Kinkade painting. He says this every Sunday.

I know it is. I know it is. I reply every Sunday. Bunni doesn't like to leave his small, cheaply built house that doesn't have central air but five air-conditioning units built into the faux-wood walls. It's too hot for him to go outside in the daylight. It's too lonely and chilling to go outside at night. The sky is too far away to look at as a pal. The stars too monstrous because they're so bright and not exhausted. Bunni's retired from working at Citgo. He cut back smoking two packs a day to a ½ a pack a day using his special 'love n' light technique' he learned from the movie. I don't ask. It will always smell like stale cigs and too much muffled heat in his house, I'm sure.

He doesn't decorate his place. He takes the five-hour trip to a thrift store in south Dallas, once a season, for new home decorations, anyways. His buddy, Bart, works there. Bart was Dad's high school friend, who is my godfather, and also is my art-dealer boss and friend, Bunni's father. Bart was also the linebacker of the Texas A&M Aggies from 1974-1978. Bart moved to Dallas after we left for New York City and after he retired from Citgo, also. Bart has massive arms that won't fit into any T-shirt, so he cuts the arms off of his t-shirts and always wears overalls. He also has a blonde buzz cut and hasn't aged since 1978 either. Anyways, Dad gets real excited about wall hangings that resemble Thomas Kinkade. So excited that he forces Bart to hide any possible Thomas Kinkade underneath a loose floorboard, under a dirty Chinese rug, at the thrift store warehouse in south Dallas until Dad can make his seasonal trek up that way. Bunni thinks every picture of a pastel house that looks like it's the home of Snow White, with a gas light in front of it and a bible quote below it, is a Thomas Kinkade.

Thomas Kinkade came to pass last year, and so Dad knows that these wall hangings'll be worth something. Dad doesn't need to be told how to turn a buck around. Looking at the warm palette of Kinkadain soft, hot pinks, midnight blues and Parisian greens is better than dealing with his alcoholism. Dad can't be the guy that he once was and likewise can't hang out with the guys he once did. Mom left him and me when I was little and moved back to her Mexican family in Queens, New York. All the rejection he's come to know in his life has made for lonesomeness, so I researched everything I could about Thomas Kinkade and Eat, Pray, Love, for that matter. Just so we can talk, forget, and laugh about things, even if it's just for a little while on Sundays.

I found out that Thomas Kinkade grew up with a poor, single ma in California like Dad who grew up with a poor, single ma in Oklahoma. I also find out that Thomas Kinkade was actually an alcoholic, too, and maybe died from it but I don't wanna tell Dad that. It might give him an excuse to break his sobriety. The body's craving for poison is the only love found-only love that sticks around. Alcohol has left him with the damned shakes and a host of intestinal, psychological and nervous system problems. All the friendships and marriages lost and loneliness that comes and stays to be absorbed by the broken, abused body is another heartache. He lives through every day. But Dad still has Bart. Dad can't imagine all the good luck a lil' love n' light has brought 'em, he's so happy!

"Good! Good! Fuck yeah! That's the spirit!" I encourage him on Sundays.

I moved to the Upper East Side six months ago to get away from all the trash/drama that seemed to precede me in the Lower East Side when I lived there for a while. I get better sleep up here and have more time to do the simple things, the healthy things in life, like brush my long, unruly hair, drink water and apply eye cream before bed. I wear a thick white satin robe in my apartment. I take walks in Central Park, eat healthy and life is good!

My neighbor across the hall, Bunni, is on disability; so she doesn't really feel up to do anything except watch daytime television, tell me about her ex-husband who funds her current operation of watching daytime television, and order take out. She tells me she's an artist and so she can't live like others. She says the word artist with a lot of dignity.

I tell her I understand completely. It's tough to feel like an outsider. Bunni has Crone's Disease and has lots of free time even with all the TV watching so she wrote a screenplay. I encourage her.

I like to relax now at night. I stay in my apartment like I'm doing tonight wearing my white satin robe. I brush my hair. It's nice and feels sweet, haimish even. A bellow of a big yell comes from the hall. Like a woman giving birth to a whole sow. I run to the door and look out the peephole.

It's my neighbor, Bunni. She's hobbling over to my door in her typical red sweatpants that are too tight and too short on her. An oversized black polyester blouse with the big happy sunflowers on it flutters around her like a mob of munchkins under a happy blanket, and cheap rubber flip-flops that make a god-awful noise, like a rat is giving birth, jealously moans with every step she takes. Its Bunni who bellows as she hobbles. We only live 14 steps from each other and, from the sounds, that's certainly enough. She has what appears to be a white box in her hands. I think about hiding, but in panic and inner commotion, I frantically throw open the door before she can even knock.

I smile and try to be social. I nervously tell her hello.

She doesn't want it.

Howd'a do? I smile like the whole of West Texas.

I ask her if she thinks it'll storm tonight, even more nervously.

She doesn't want that, either.

She drops the box at her flip-flops and grabs both of my wrists firmly. I gasp. I yell-whisper, Dio unconsciously. Her hands are uncannily warm, almost perspiring. She pleads I help her. She's gasping for air.

"She's on to something big!" She lips without speaking.

She speaks about herself in third person singular. She questions the validity of her identity as "I" because she's an artist.

Bunni conspiratorially leans in closer to me, and I smell that she's been eating enough Oreo cookies and vanilla icing but she gets in closer, and closer until her mouth is in my hair and she gasps, "…something big…real-flippin-big… about…." She pauses.

I let her. She has done this before, and I smell artificial vanilla made in corporate cookie factories, "…humanity!"

She is practically howling at me and says humanity like it's the waters of immortality and she just got the first, free sip from The Lord.

She's done with her screenplay. Her mood, I understand, is a sort of VIP celebration where she's the only one privy to such an ecstatic, rare party. I let her have it. Everybody's the same, you know.

Party on Bunni, Party on.

Bunni wants me to edit the damned thing.

"How long is it?" I ask, as I release myself from her grip.

"Only rrrr----pages." She says as she laboriously bends down to pick up the box.

"What?" I say. "I didn't hear you."

"I said it's only 734!!!! Pages!!! 734! GLORIOUS! PAGES!!!" She screams rudely, her face muggy and red from all the aerobics that she has now performed.

"It'll take you no time," she says. I'm blown back and excuse myself as I can't work for free, anymore. It hasn't looked so good on me. I explain. She tells me that she has Crone's Disease, again.

I don't say nothing. She does something weird with her feet and it causes her rubber flip-flop to make another rat-birthing gasp. We both get uncomfortable. I straighten my spine and put my hands behind my back. I tell her to have a good night. Bunni doesn't leave before she manically shoves 730 or so pages of loose leaf paper in my apartment. She nearly bruised my hip shoving it in here. She runs away from me, desultorily, and cautiously looks back every three or so steps away, all the while panting. It takes her enough time to get back to her apartment because she's so sick. She slams her door.

I look down at her sloppy masterpiece spilled everywhere. It's clean white pages with black type on it like so much senseless, manmade fuckedness. The squeaky sound of her flip-flops seems to reverberate through the windowless hallway for the twenty minutes it takes me, bent down, to order the pages correctly. Later that night, after I finish brushing my hair, I tug it into a braid and sweep it in a bun on top of my head like a little crown. I apply eye cream. I drink a glass of high alkaline and mineralized water and read the first three pages since I'm now her pro-bono editor.

It begins with two 'sultry' sisters 'with 1950's pinup bodies (but NOT fat)' it says clearly in parentheses. They are yelling at each other over an old Christina Aguillera song that comes on the radio. Bunni didn't specify what song.

Sister 1: 'We had sex together…one last passionate night!...before he made his little proposition. To think, he's sixty-five and still an attentive lover!

(The younger sister applauds wildly)

Sister 2: "What a wonderful life it will be for you!"

(The younger sister pauses. Pauses like a gasp. They listen to Christina Aguillera)

Sister 2: "You could have all the money you'd ever spend!...It would be like life at the White House!...But only better! Because he wouldn't nag you on what to spend!...He would give you the world!...Forget about your Crone's Disease! You could put your arms out and take off your blouse, laugh, laugh darling, topless, and dance, dance, dance!"

I'm pleasantly horrified by Bunni's screenplay. It's basically like Little Women, but better because death isn't the only enemy that can really kill a girl. It's terrifically anti-intellectual. It's plain, honest and morbid. A new sense of pain invades the groundwork of my heart.

Bunni is spreading her illness! But it won't sell. Nobody takes this shit seriously. There's other people with hotter shit to take seriously. The thing about Bunni is that she identifies herself through her pain. Anybody who reads her screenplay will also identify with pain and illness, and then they will identify with each other, as a community of humans, regardless if their name is Bunni, Catholic, art dealer, abuelita, Dad, or 5-DhW. What humility, courage and insignificance in Pure-T crap! What a world!

I just broke up with my boyfriend, Bunni. Bunni moved back to his parent's cattle ranch in the flatlands of West Texas. They own the biggest ranch there is out there, so it's a comfortable place to be. He says that since he moved away (we lived together in the Lower East Side) he enjoys going to bed much later than we used to. He sleeps better. He has a new girlfriend. Bunni's new girlfriend looks like Iggy Pop and I'm not just saying that because I don't like her. I never liked her because she's the type of girl that's always swaying around like she's drunk in love when any, and I mean any, boy is around. You know the type that moves in quick and will date just about anybody's boyfriend. Just as long as it's somebody else's boyfriend.

The important thing is that they identify themselves, and each other, through the lenses of their illness. It holds the gd thing together. But to not be a Bunni?

I rest my head on Bunni's 700 +page screenplay about humanity. I'm laughing and crying because I don't want to think about how desperate it all is, but I'm sorta messing up the printed black words with my tears. The important thing is that they persistently identify themselves through their illness.

How long will it last?

Is it medieval to treat concepts as a bad illness that only a holy woman can correct?

GOD DIDN'T GIVE YOU A FACE LIKE THAT FOR NO REASON.

It was winter. I was really down and out, working three shitty jobs and still not being able to pay my rent in Brooklyn. I called my Dad back in West Texas. I asked if he'd let me borrow 500 dollars and promised to pay back in six months.

He sighed heavily into the phone. It sounded like hissing. He didn't say nothing.

From my cell phone's ear receiver, I could hear the desolate sound of wind rolling through the flat, brown field beyond Dad's house and rattling the dull, slate blue siding of his house. Beyond that, a rusty barbed wire fence that needed repairs. Beyond the barbed wire was a larger brown lot. A couple of cattle stood. No grass to graze. It was quiet, embarrassing and lonely. Funny to think that I can hear and see all of this from a couple of tiny holes in a cell phone. Outside, in Brooklyn it was snowing heavily.

He still said nothing.

"Well, what is it! I'm not made to feel guilty. I'm doing the best I can. Can you help?" I blurted out when I thought of the cattle.

"Daughter, no. No." He sounded annoyed. "The Lord didn't give you a face like that for no reason."

It was quiet. I imagined the low gusts of winter wind towering in high flung currents beyond Dad's field. Those vicious sweeps of wind that would rattle the house. Once, I hoped that the wind would swoop me outta there to New York City, or somewhere. Hell if I cared where. Anywhere. I didn't say anything or ask what he meant by what he said. I knew what he meant. God didn't give me a face like that for no reason.

My face was pretty. Pretty is a free pass. I could ride all I wanted. I could take the ride over and over again, so many damned times I could ride but I could never get off. I could ride through a fatherless land of dirty, cold sidewalks holding the hard footsteps coming from suits with big gold watches. If you had a decent enough face the kids back home and all your fancy new city friends, equally could follow your exciting existence on Instagram. They'd have that sorta option. That was a good outcome in life. To be followed on social media. To be called pretty. I was probably trying to kill myself and make it seem like a part girl's accident. I drank so much that I fainted at work yesterday. I didn't mind it so much. I wanted to get off the ride.

Dad sighed heavily again. I told him thanks anyways. Sorry to bother him.

We hung up. I looked out the tiny window that looked down into a tinier patch of sidewalk hidden by dirty snow and brick buildings. Snow fell sideways as people with hats, umbrellas, giant puffy coats and galoshes quickly scuttled by. I couldn't see one face. Everyone scurried around like they just learned how to walk and were blind. I felt blind too.

Dad, the whole world is blind and running. And I'm there too, and so are you. You're blinded by your homegrown ethics, the American dream and your chain emails of cuddly puppies that you forward me every three months. "Live simply, love each moment," written like it's a lesson to be learned. A lesson for cute puppies who exist on the surface of mass-produced greeting cards. Living simply like that. Living simply is the elevated shopping mall for rich girls who have other options. The snow fell in a directionless fury like it was making a dumb, scattered and futureless choice.

Now that I'm here in Brooklyn, where I wanted to wind up, I prefer the cattle with the sad eyes. Their large, thrashed out bodies have no space for such cheap and cruel slogans. There's all sorts of ways to be blind. And then, to escape, run around bumping into furniture that will outlast your bruised and bloody legs. I put my hot cheek on the cold windowpane and began crying.

Spring came. I go on dates with all sorts of old farts my father's age. Hey, at least I eat now. I've quit two of my jobs.

I've gained the weight back. All the steak, chocolate and wine have lent me a little more weight. My midsection, upper hips and lower breasts seem engorged, protecting me--- but I can't say what I'm being protected from though. Or why a girl without many choices would need anything safe and warm. They say that the grass is greener on the other side of the fence. They say that the darkest hour is just before dawn. They say that a lady wears her tears like jewelry.

Let 'em fucking have it. Let them put it on a Hallmark card or a facebook post. Let them talk all about it. I wish I wasn't a poor pretty girl at all. I wish I was a bull. Chewing apathetically on tiny purple flowers in a land I'll never know the name to, or care about the names to, anyways.

God didn't give me a face like this for no reason.

CHRISTMAS, 1809, OR WAS IT 1709?

How are we supposed to know who's underneath this crust of earth if they don't even have a name on their gravestone? Everyone has a name on their gravestone. Everyone. Except one in the town's graveyard where I live.

Listen, all I'm saying is this: when you're alive you can do all sorts of things: you can fly a kite. Or wonder why people fly kites. Or what's so damned fun about flying a kite, anyways? You could charge people money so they can fly a kite.

That's what I liked to do in a metaphorical way. Make people fly a kite. So, I got into politics. Now that I'm old and about to die, I know that my life has been funneled into a silly straw hole and all I can do is suck from the name of 'Governor'. I slurped stupidly in a starched dress shirt. If I stopped sucking and looked up, it was only to foresee possible future financial gains and not look at the sky.

Since death is near and I was taught as a Methodist that heaven was up I really look up. I do other things than look up. I do things I normally wouldn't do. I look around, really look around. I touch trees. It's really just one beautiful old tree that sits in the middle of the community cemetery that I touch. Yesterday, I even cried while I touched this tree, even though I touch it mostly every day.

I cried while I was touching this tree because it felt like some hard boot came out of nowhere, divorced from a body, just a mean boot with a strong, sturdy kick and kicked me right in the heart. It bust something inside of me and left my body like a splintered, rotting doorframe. Have you ever felt like that? Have you ever loved like that? My heart was bruised and broken and it didn't stop there, I realized that everything I once depended on, my name, my experiences, my money was just another lie. I grabbed my raw heart and looked at the earth through my tears. God, I went home limping and quiet after that one. I understand tree huggers now. I do.

Listen, I take a walk in the graveyard because there are never too many people there. I like to go on quiet walks without addling my senses with the apposite rules of social propriety such as saying, 'Hey! How do you do? And Good Evening, Governor!' I enjoy daydreaming, uninterruptedly. I walk and dream. Certainly, it behooves me to be impolite or considered gauche, so I go to the graveyard. No one is there. No one asks me to join them in the hearty game of social propriety or for an afternoon coffee and pie. I walk laps but the graveyard is large, miles wide and miles long and I'm old. Once, when walking on the far north end of the graveyard, I heard a lovely rustic whistling from the middle. In the distance, over a small hill, I saw a mulberry tree and I walked over. It took me at least forty minutes to get there.

It was around 5:30 pm when I got under the tree. The shade was so sweet and cool you would think seraphim were dozing in and out of sleep. The smell of wet bark, untouched earth and lovable, tiny flowers in a cool dew enchanted me. I decided to sit down against the trunk of the tree. I sat there for a while and regained my strength. The light became dusty and I felt so happy and bubbly that I actually dozed off. When I woke up again it was dark, in the middle of the night, and I was freezing with a cold I had never felt before. Cold, that seemed to come from my bones, rather than the air. For a while, I rummaged my hand inside my coat, around my heart to find a heartbeat. I couldn't find one. Quickly and groggily, I got up and began running as fast as I could manage. I thought that I was a ghost so I wanted to run again. Run like I was strong and young, again. My heart was beating so fast. I had not run in decades. Nothing like this has ever happened to me. I only ran twelve long dashes before I toppled over something and moaned.

My shins felt like they had exploded against something very tough, tougher than my old bones. I didn't want to yell. What if there were robbers around? My heart began to beat so fast that it stopped. I thought this is it. I am dying. I thought, what a terrific way to die! On the cold dark earth, alone with your legs so mangled and broken that you know, for sure, you're meant to be right here as you are. Can't run around anymore. Legs, useless. Movement, what's the point? Now, it's time to really go somewhere. I tried to calm myself down but it was a new moon and very dark and the darkness seemed to make slippery shapes around me. The darkness gave me an energy to get up, get up goddamnit! But I couldn't. I knew even if I did get up, I still had over an hour to walk before I even got out of the graveyard.

My shins hurt so bad that I couldn't get up. I began crawling. Crawling like I used to as a baby, over the expanse of the graveyard. It took me nearly three hours until I was finally safe, out of the darkness and in the sneering, government-provided fluorescent copper street lights. It was morning by the time I got home. I got very sick after that and everyone thought that I was a goner but I knew I wasn't. I had no such luck. I had survived three wars, was The General of two of them, and spent forty years in public office. I had skin to make a baseball glove balk. I had the unluck of surviving, of having tough bones. The hurt that turns you hard from seeing sorrow, pain and death and wars, to see man-inflicted sorrow, pain and manufactured war for so many long, long years. I knew under the earth were buried many men, many friends that died because of me, the nature of war.

The next month, after my health returned, I went back to the cemetery with slightly bruised shins and the end of a whooping cough to see if I could find what caused me to fall. What was tougher than my own bones? What had the power to make an old curmudgeon/veteran/ex-Governor and General like me fall? What force, what awful force made me realize that my life was a war-like lie and that to really look up, one must look down, way down. Terrible anatomy!

I walked with a cane for an hour. I saw the mulberry tree. I walked around and took my time. Under another tree, I found this gravestone that said, 'Christmas 1809' or '1709', it was hard to tell. The 8 or the 7 was smudged into oblivion on the white marble. The crumbled white marble no bigger than an attacking possum, it looked that way too-but even eerier because it didn't move. All the other gravestones had names but not this one, and I began going there every day. I had a cute wicker chair placed by the crumbled gravestone that looked like an attacking possum. Christmas, eternally Christmas.

The days passed. I was bothered by the one gravestone that didn't have a name on it. Why was she alone? Why was she so lucky to not have a name on her gravestone? Was she so above names that only a holiday could describe her heart and cheer? Was she freed from the descriptive lies that I had to live, live through my skin, that I was buried under? Why did she get the best spot in the dead joint?

Life transcends what your loved ones will say about you at your funeral or what's engraved on your gravestone. Life is more than your great, or lousy, personality and all the noisy deserving, or noisy not deserving you get. More than victories of war or the everyday business of war. One didn't have to be popular to be given life. One didn't even need to be given a name to be a source of inspiration, light and comfort-and this gravestone became that to me.

We never speak of the life available to us, the raw, silent life that comes to us in our last days on earth. The pulse of extraordinary life pumping from the earth, from this ordinary crust of soil. Any touch, the tree, the wind seemed to puncture me into soup. If I was a baby, I would loaf around screaming with this wild energy. Life gives her strangest and most benevolent fruits at the moment it seems to be utterly defeated, yeah, crushed.

I had these thoughts at her grave, actually. I felt that it was the subtle vibrations of her decomposed body radiating through my winter boots, pervading my cozy wool socks to the soles of my feet and up the prodigious climb through my bones, to my rational mind that lent such thoughts to me. Life and death were so close I didn't know how they were separate. Everything rose and flourished and felt defeated but being defeated like this was better than being victorious. I had never felt defeated. There were roots here, roots inside the earth, and inside our bodies, in the living and the dead, in dying and those full of life, invisible, yet palpable, and she was meshed in this world. Her body had gone. It didn't matter what name was rubbed out of her gravestone. Maybe somewhere she was a girl, again.

She was dead, yes, but she had become a cool spring of new life, lush water, in my bruised, brittle heart. Christmas for a little boy. I decided that we were pals of sorts. She was certainly a strange pal to give me, a mean geezer and ruthless General, such insights about life from a place of immaterial decomposition.

Two months have passed and I haven't died yet. Now, in spring, I still go there every day mostly. I find it peaceful, actually. In all sorts of unpredictable weather, I cared only about going to see the unknown lady died Christmas 1809 or 1709. It's hard to tell the numbers are so worn. Maybe it's a man buried here? I wouldn't care.

Now that she's alive in my heart, my family doesn't like me walking in graveyards. They don't like that I plan to build her a better grave. They say it's a waste of money. My new investments have caused such stupid gossip. As if this dead woman, this erased grave was a hot, wet panty- and it's always a panty that causes empiric demise. If they insist on panties to manipulate an old man, then I shall say that her metaphysical panty kicked off the dust and fustiness in my old heart, pumped it full of warm blood and wet desire and sent my tongue salivating for New Life. So how bad can such a panty be?

The truth is her body was elsewhere, her panties too. The living's greed makes even dead, decomposing things a threat. Not that she was thinking of anything, not a deeper ocean or a better man to love. Or a warmer place on this earth. I gave. Not because I had to, but because I was compelled to. Not that she wanted a better gravestone but I began the rudimentary architectural planning to fashion her with a new one to give to her, anyways.

Of course, they whisper. The whole town whispers, let them. I'm crazy enough not to care. By summer, the completion of an exact replica of the Taj Mahal on the four acres of land, by the mulberry tree, is now hers, in her honor-this nobody woman. By this in memoriam mento wonderland, I serve free pancake breakfasts to the community. Yes, under the mulberry tree, every Thursday, from sunrise to sundown. I serve all.

Mortuary pancakes, I kid around. I'm now the proprietor, and CEO, of The Taj Mahal of Pancakes. We have four locations around our county and there are talks for statewide expanding. On Thursdays, pancakes, all you can eat non-GMO pancakes, made from farm fresh eggs and buttermilk are on the house. So is the coffee, thick and bitter. Besides, it's nice to eat home cooked pancakes with all walks and casts of life, in an exact replica of The Taj Mahal. We're not IHOP, we're The Taj Mahal of Pancakes which happenstance, is much superior than an international pancake.

Three years have passed. I'm 98 now. It's winter again. I understand love, to give and receive love is life's only miracle, and some of us, yes, the fortunate ones, are lucky to find the whole world in our beloved. To love someone so thoroughly that there's no damned qualms about including everyone, every sonabitch and saint, in that love. It makes time silly. It makes money silly. It makes all sorts of things that I thought hard and tough, silly and sweet like maple syrup.

There's no you anymore, you see. No her, no world. Yesterday, the blue sky was mottled in orange Rorschach perversity. The sky looked like a massive tie-dyed shirt, underneath her mini-replica of The Taj Mahal. A few leaves stuck to the branches of the tree and rattled in a low wind. I carefully went over the raised platform architecture and let my eyes wonder to the forecourt. When my eyes reached the carving of mythical flowers, inlaid stone, blue mosaics, and semiprecious stones of cornelian, coral and onyx, I jumped. There, in the inner octagon of carved white marble screens, was a note under a smooth stone the size of a fist. The note had my name on it.

No one knows my real name, actually. I had it changed when I became a famous politician back in the 1970's. Alarmed, I looked around. One can imagine how alarmed I was. No one knew my real name. Nobody alive. My heart beat faster and I felt a lump in my throat as I stared at that hateful handwriting with my real name on it. The new note responded by shaking gently, together with me, in a cold wind. There was no one around.

I was shaken up so much I could barely reach my weak arm out to pick it up. Taking off a mitten, I opened it. There was nothing written on it. I folded up the paper, put it in my coat pocket and walked home.

That night I dreamt about a kiss that was thick with warm lips, wet with saliva and salt water tears. Like it meant, I forgive you. I don't give a rat's ass about what you did in the past. I love ya' any old ways. And soon I was dreaming of other things. Like all the people I used to know, some died in war far away from home. The ones that survived aren't there anymore, either. You're somewhere else, too. They don't know what you are becoming. And you miss them. There's not even a gravestone to mark their passing.

There's an ache. The next day I came back to the grave. In the inner octagon of carved white marble screens was another stone. The stone held another piece of paper with my name on it. There was no one around. Taking off my mitten, I opened it. There was nothing written on it. I folded up the paper, put it in my pocket, and walked home.

The next day I came back to the grave. There was another piece of paper there. There was no one around. Taking off my mitten, I opened it. There was nothing written on it. I understood enough to know I'd never really know. I folded up the paper and walked home. I fell. I got up. I fell. I didn't get up.

There was no use in putting anything in my pockets, anymore.

MIAMI HOTEL.

The fancy boy wants me to stay here and doesn't see why I can't live at The Hotel in Miami without Mommy. The bedspread is patterned with bright green palm leaves sprinkled on eggshell white. It's so soft that I lie on it without caring about the germs others have left. Usually, I think of germs in hotels. I don't care how nice the hotel is, everybody leaves germs. The air outside is heavy, hot and the sky a glorified blue. Yachts are parked in the bay. Some yachts sail slowly out toward deeper, bluer water. I don't like explaining myself to him, so what's there to discuss? We live on different planets, really. It's strange we're even in the same room together.

I didn't want to say goodbye to Mommy. She didn't want to stay here on this rich kid's dime. She was a grown-ass woman, she said. She didn't feel right about it, she said. Moms the only one who I've known for this long, all nineteen years of my life, and I love her so much, it makes my stomach feel queasy, like I'll just turn into homesickness, a milkshake or confetti, even. I can't think of how I'll feel when she leaves. She always ends up leaving, though, and I drink for a while, crying and avoiding everyone like I do now.

There's no need for a glass. I drink bourbon outta the bottle. I don't even go swimming in the ocean anymore and I love swimming in the ocean. I have less than 30 dollars to my name. Mom got another credit card and lives in a nice condo in California and three days ago she called to tell me that the heel of her fancy shoe broke and that it'll cost more than 400 dollars to repair! Why, my word! I thought. That hunk of shoe costs more than I'm worth.

That's all we talk about. The broken stuff of life. Of course, he's got all sorts of healthy opinions about this. He tells me she doesn't really care about me. I shrug him off. He's using his unbroken, rich boy logic but what does that matter to me? He doesn't know what it is to really be free. To live with your heart like a bird, so free and high above the dogshit and yachts of this claustrophobic world. So free to sail beyond the window, beyond land, beyond the troubled water to deeper sea. To live everyday like that. What would that be like? Never remembering the bad memories. Never thinking it's bad enough to start telling yourself stories about the good memories.

To let go in this freedom, to just let go. To know it so well that even the pretty, rich things look like only a bad hair extension job. He doesn't know what it is to love like that. To prefer to be bald than given a bad extension job. He doesn't know what it is to be a daughter who loves their only parent, Mother, so much just saying 'Mother' makes you want to cry and there's a lump in your chest and you turn to a milkshake inside.

He is going on and on, and on and on, about how mom is a selfish woman. I take another swig. Who cares huh? He keeps it up until I've reached my limit.

"I don't give a fart what you say! You talk…an…an..all I smell is all dem farts coming out of your mouth, anyways."

He doesn't like it when I talk like a man and I get embarrassed.

"I'm a lousy drunk anyways, so better let the dead bury the dead!"

He keeps talking it sounds like wonk-wonk-wonk like Charlie Brown hears in the classroom talk. I can't take the lecturing sound.

"Leave me be!!!!"

He says something else but I don't hear him because I scream as loud as I can.

"GET OUT!!!!" I scream. "Get out!!!" I scream, again. And I mean it, too. He does. He doesn't like to make a scene. It bothers him. Making scenes. I know this and use this as my desperate ace. He's all hemmed in by boring outfits like socially acceptable behavior but at least he feels the touch of something, even if it is just a hem. Just seams. I cry again, cry like I lost my mom, a god-awful, lonely and miserable cry.

The fancy boy comes back in the door and grabs his phone and wallet and leaves again. I stop crying. I don't want anyone to hear me like that. Besides, what's the point of crying like I'm 100 years old to a boy who acts like he's 100 hours old?

In this hotel in Miami the bathroom mirror even has a TV in it. What does it matter if I'm in or I'm out, if TVs are in the mirror?? Can I ever get away from their fat opinions? The quiet sets into the hotel room again. I pretend that I'm normal. Normal, like him, no need to go to shatters! No need to go to shatters, no need to go to shatters. I repeat it over and over again in a hotel room that is getting smaller and smaller. No need to go to shatters, I whisper now, again and again. My skull and lips are throbbing, numb. I can't feel my body.

The colors are so bold here in Miami, inside this hotel and outside the window, I get nauseated and try to stand up. I can't. I fall by the bed. I don't see the point of going outside. I grab the bedspread and use it to pull me back up to where I was lying on the bed. I roll on the bed. The flush of the air-conditioning turns on. I see the remote and think I'm turning on the television. I try to find the classic cartoon network. Instead I look at the soft bedspread with the tree patterns on it. I move through the patterns.

Closer and closer enough to color blocks, and then colored threads. All a very soft surface. Soft, soft, soft…soft…I whisper like a lullaby to myself. I know that peace shall make its home in even my heartbeat. My window shattering heartbeat.

IT WAS A TIME WHEN THE LAND WAS SOFT AS WET CARPET.

It was a happy time. It was a time when the land was soft as wet carpet. He was a senior in high school. Two weeks ago, he had been offered a full scholarship to play college football some four states away in Oklahoma, and that very same day, he had been offered to just go ahead, skip college, go straight to the pros in his home state, too.

He was one of the blessed, he knew. His mother and sisters wouldn't have to suffer anymore; he was going to be paid. He picked the pros and The Jacksonville Jaguars was a nice team. That way he could be close to his mother and sisters. That way life would be about the same and get better, at the same time.

When the land was soft as wet carpet he didn't give a damn if he could play football or what day it was, or what season it was, or what was going on around him or what color his skin was; he was so happy. He didn't care about anything. He was a child of the sun! The only thing that made him happy wasn't football but soft mud that your feet melted into. It was mud of the swamplands. His home. The only land he knew. A sinking soil that sunk anybody, with any title, with it.

Every Sunday, he got to the large church complex early, rolled up his dress pants, took of his comfortable church shoes and socks, neatly placed them on the beige car rug, by the driver's car seat, and set off barefoot into the woods. He took a walk where there was nobody. He liked the way the land felt under his feet, soft as wet carpet.

He went to one cool place where it was always muddy. He would stand in the dense mud gleefully, like it was a footbath of high-grade drugs made to relax and elevate him. And as he felt so elevated, he watched everybody from his town arrive at church in the tall noon sunlight that cast pine tree shadows on all.

For the normal to seem bizarre, he had to move further away from the familiar, while still being close enough to be a part of it all. He stood with mud on his feet. He pretended as if he was crushing wet grapes under his feet, and then, wiggled his feet around until they were fully submerged in the cool, thick substance. He watched the normal people filing into the mega-church. He pretended he was a wine-maker-monk in Italy! He could say 'Ciao Life!' and not care if anybody answered back, not cared if anybody thought he had lost his damned mind in the mud.

Ciao, Life! Sometimes, he thought that the mud must be color of his true love's hair. The girl he would love forever had hair the rich color of wet tree bark. Nobody knew what he pretended. Nobody knew he was there. It was good to be this far away. It was good to have a shallow buffer of pine trees between you and everybody else. Good to watch the shape of the shadows flutter over people's bodies in the sunshine.

Four years went by. Life was about the same but much better. He played professional football. He still went to church. He still walked privately to the woods and let his feet soak in the mud. He still thought about how lucky he was to be alive in the mud. 15 minutes before church was to begin, he walked back to his car, the way that nobody else walked, where there was no path, kinda wiped off his feet, threw his socks on, laced up his church shoes, and rushed into church, smiling, and perhaps making some rushed small talk with some fellow church members. He liked being around all the people he knew since forever, in a mega-building established solely for worshiping the holy, with a secret mud caked on his feet. The mud made the preacher's words all the more tolerable. The mud made him feel like he was light as a seagull's feather even though he was the biggest guy at church.

And what was the cause of such highness? It wasn't anything that anybody else knew about. It was mud. Just mud. Malleable soil that was from the dirty bottom of the earth, a substance so low there was no other name for it but mud. Mud. Shit. Barefoot. He was delighted.

Otherwise, without the mud, the whole church thing became depressing. He felt like he was at a multi-media karaoke mega-event for squares where everything was being taped for TV. There was that sort of phony anticipation in the air, phony cheer, those sorta phony interactions between mostly regular people.

Things changed at church in other ways. The high-tech, million-dollar light system that the church recently installed added a new horror to the whole show. At the proper crescendos of the loud rock music, from a large and growing rock band (five electric bass players, three drummers with full drum sets, four lead acoustic guitarists and eight singers) the colored lights and lasers seized happily but everything- the music, lights, singers were screaming. At that high moment, the eight singers, with mostly fat arms, raised their hands as if they were searching for an invisible cookie jar too far above their heads. Their eyes were closed. Their fat arms jiggled. The people in the audience had their eyes closed. From at least forty feet high, the lights wrenched marine blue to pulsating hot pink, to a steady, bright, Peter Pan green while the noise, the fucking noise of Christian radio music came to life and grinded across the smooth cross. The cross remained understated, Christ-less and white. Very white.

Everyone bellowed, together, eyes closed, reaching and drenched in color lights. What was the cause of such inverted highness? Christ. God. Clothes and Shoes on. He couldn't close his eyes. This whole powerhouse of gesture and song was drenched in an artificial, terror-alert green that made the giant room flip-flop and spin in an individualized, unmerciful and visceral subordination.

In the cacophony of high-tech color, music and message, his fellow church members cried. Cried in joy, cried in Jesus Lives, Jesus Saves. They touched their hearts and raised their hands at about the same time, too. They couldn't help it. In such emotional, transcendental almost telepathic spins the supremacy of the unadorned white cross was the only safe anchor to plug one's eyes into.

He stared at the cross. He began to cry, too. But his tears seemed to be pouring from a much different source than everyone else's tears. He cried because he felt alone. He felt panic. He'd always been this way. Just feeling alone.

What was real and fiercely true for others was a cheap karaoke show where everybody was worse than carrying about shitfaced stinko, they were sober. Sober in headache colors doing their thing. It lasted thirty minutes or a bit more. Why was he condemned not to feel the love of God with everybody else, too? Why was he exempt?

Why couldn't he feel free? He was alone. A mutant with brown mud on his feet that a smooth white cross couldn't save. The lights never were brown or black. This happened every week. It was the same. It was so the same it seemed dubious. He thought that the people that he'd known since forever weren't people after all. They were robots. It wasn't a comforting explanation. But it seemed to make sense. Like everybody had a computer chip in their brains that made them feel high and holy for thirty minutes or so, underneath the prerequisite conditions of Sunday worship at The Mega-Church. All the tears from what a day, all the compliant days, had done to a spirit. All the misguided feelings from all the days, the long, humid Florida days, wrapped up with lights, gay music and tears until this psycho-spiritual goulash chained everybody together as one. When this computer chip highness wasn't there he had witnessed them too: they were normal, formulaic and successful business people. Their talk was the shits, for sure.

The preacher was nearly 50 but he looked like a 20-year old model selling jeans in a JC Penney's catalogue. He came on stage after the music was over like he was running victoriously onto a football field through the sounds of everybody crying. The preacher's charisma and presentation seemed more important than his message. His favorite theme was on 'downloads from the Lord' and 'marketing for Jesus'. It was taught that Christ from Nazareth was also the CEO of American Capitalism.

It was a message for people trapped from the inside. They had changed since he went to the pros. Now, they wanted to include him and his mother and his sisters. His family was invited to all sorts of places. Cheap thrills.

The company of the holy was found in the mud. But he cried more, he didn't know what was happening to him. He even saw it on the football field. He would look up, way passed his team members, the cheerleaders, referees, coaches and camera people at the stands full of blurry dark people. He couldn't make out one face in the lights. It was the crowd he played for. He was paid. Paid to play for them. Everybody was suffering. He played. He wore a facemask and helmet. He could only hear his breathing. He felt anonymous under all the padding, like he didn't matter at all. He just played. They watched.

Nothing to it. Before every game and sometimes during the game he would think of Job's words he had read once like a longing. Is not man's life on earth a drudgery? Are not his days those of hirelings? He is a slave who longs for the shade, a hireling who waits for his wages.

He was no different. He felt like a bar bitch, worse, a salesman. Like everybody had cheap shit in their hearts instead of having a heart made of flesh and muscle, at all. He was good at football and by the end of four years he had won MVP four times. More people shouted his name. More people tried to get close to his mother and sisters.

Are not his days those of hirelings? He went out into the mud. Now the mud reminded him that only the surface of the earth was measured in miles. So much of life: an unnecessary fucking strain of numbers, distinctions, variations to feel proud or accomplished over. It was a typical visit to this sick karaoke house. Everywhere was a sick karaoke house.

That year, as some friends from the church settled down for marriage and babies, he settled down for a siege of schizophrenia. Earlier in the year, an insane fan raped and murdered his mother and three sisters.

He quit football the next day. He wanted to quit life, too. He moved out of his mansion into a new apartment complex where his uncle lived. When it wasn't Sunday there was dread in daily, mindless chores like brushing his teeth or putting the silver car key in the ignition and turning. The mechanical cacophony under the hood of his mass-produced jalopy seemed to jeer at him. The feel of the toothbrush on his teeth was too abrasive.

Everything that he loved was gone, worse than gone, beaten and bloodied, dead, dead, dead. Mutilated and abused. There was a hole inside. And that tragedy fell and fell and fell through that hole so many times, so many fucking times, that he knew this hole in his heart didn't have a bottom. It was deeper than the earth. That's what it felt like inside, like every moment a hole deeper than the earth was ripping him up inside. His guilt, remorse and responsibility were never-ending as never-ending as that inverted repulsive hole. It was his fault.

He gave away all his fancy cars. He went back to driving the car that his uncle had bought him when he turned sixteen. He had kept it as a souvenir from his old life. That car, a 2001 Mazda Protégé, meant more to him than anything he could buy with his salary. His uncle worked over 300 hours to buy him that car. It would take him 3 seconds to buy that car with his football salary. Cheap shit. All around him, cheap shit.

All his thoughts had a gloom to them, like the shadow was on the inside, like the shadow wouldn't budge. The dread of knowing that the heart will beat on and on regardless of if you want it to or not. Dread, the everyday variety. He got a new kitten and named him Percy Mae so he could touch something soft and new. He took 12 prescription pills a day. He doped out. Mystery took energy. Living took energy. Putting his feet in the mud took energy. He had none. He stopped going outside. He never wanted to go to the grocery store, or play a game, or go to the barber's ever again. He wanted to go somewhere far away and sink in the mud there.

He thought about suicide a lot. He felt shy about it. He already didn't have many people to confide in. Sure, the good members of Port City Community Church would come by, not on church days, and try their best to aid their fellow church member back to health.

They wanted to talk football and not rape or mental illness and who could blame 'em? There was nothing to say about the unrecoverable loss of his beloved mom and sisters. Nothing to say when shit got really, really bad. There was much to say about the possibilities for joy now, and the spiritual and mental fortitude that could spring from such a tremendous loss. But possibility wasn't actuality. They spoke about new life in the codified way.

Solutions, like worries, are of the mind. Made up as a thought or a wish. They wanted to give him solutions. The more pragmatic the better. A guidebook for the cheerfulness, happiness and gratitude they all partook in. He considered it.

He tried to consider it but they seemed like strangers to him, even though he knew them since forever. He was humiliated when they came to his apartment. He was more humiliated when they sat in mauve plastic chairs in his living room and performed cheerfulness as they looked around at how he didn't own anything that they could see. Except the two plastic chairs. He could have picked those up outside any gas station around Jacksonville. They unfortunately thought the two chairs were code though: when you are poor, you were really being punished. He must have done something to get to be this way. The higher you fall, the more undercover wrong you had done to fall like that. Their logic, their obsessions, and worse, their love depressed him. It was just another way to get high while feeling high about yourself, about the water-downed prosperity you had in your bank account, which directly correlated with the amount of peace, the peace of Jesus, they had in their calculated, neurotic biznis-minded, football-talkin hearts. Everybody else got what they deserved.

His politeness was unwavering. The visitor's cheerfulness was unwavering, also. Except for those two seconds of disgust where their eyes swept the empty room and landed on those two mauve plastic chairs.

Those chairs made his visitors unhappy. From them, he had to look very carefully at his unhappiness. He thought that the cure was there, where no one else would dare to go. No one was going to do it for him. He had to cure himself. Soon, he was looking very carefully at every visitor's unhappiness. That quick moment when everything was real, when their eyes touched the chairs. A moment without pretense, inside, inside of course without word to it.

Outside their hair was always cut. You could see the scissor's blunt lines in their hair, men and women alike. It cut him more. His heart was a sad, squalid and abused home but he knew he wasn't so different than them.

The chair squeaked under his newly gained weight from the medication, all the not moving. Percy Mae, his new kitty, ran away when a visitor opened the door too dramatically on his way out.

At night, there was no break. He woke every thirty minutes crying for his mother and sisters. He went back to sleep with such a sour ache in his stomach, chest and throat that he tasted gasoline, metals. Maybe he had a permanent fever. Dreams were beaten down dogs, caged, and waiting for death, a clean antiseptic death at the local SPCA.

During the day, women visitors had legs like humid lust and they seemed to suck in the cheap walls of his squalid home like a fever. Like each pair of legs were the landlords of chintzy building, wanting only rent $ and then, more $, $$ & $, his heart congealing into gobs of melting butter. And a fever dream.

And more fevers. Something had to stop. He stopped taking all the pills. Weeks went by, months left too.

They were having a church get together on this Saturday night. Jennifer Cupalane, another visitor from church, told him. She wore pink nurse's scrubs and white sneakers. Jennifer was studying to be a nurse now. They went to high school together even though they didn't speak in high school. She had the most beautiful hair in high school. She was a cheerleader, popular enough and he was not a cheerleader and unpopular enough to be ignored except by the way he played football.

Now her long hair was gone. She was five years older. She had freshly cut, shoulder length brunette hair that she flat ironed, so the cut was even more severe. Under her hair was a wide face with an upturned nose and two large front teeth, like a cute Disney rendition of a mouse.

"Did you hear me, Duane? Didya? The church is having a get together this Saturday night?!" Jennifer gasped dumbly.

He looked at the large diamond on her finger. She had recently got engaged to her high school sweetheart, Tim, a man of God who wanted to passionately serve Christ and otherwise rather dispassionately took over his father's auto mall. The sound of the heater flushed on and warmed the empty room.

He shrugged and replied, "Well, maybe I'll come."

It sounded noncommittal. She wouldn't accept that.

"But leaping lizards, Duane! You can't go out on Saturday night!" She optimistically said from her thin lips.

She moved a bit in her plastic chair. It was too hot in his apartment and she smelled of fake flowers and rotten citrus. The warm smell of her vagina, like a sleepy stew made by wood trolls wafted it's comfortable and natural song into his nose. He sneezed and avoided eye contact.

"But you can't go out Saturday night!" She repeated, just as brightly. "You don't have anything to wear!" She laughed.

The pain was ambiguous. He was both nauseated and felt a sharp headache. It was unbearably hot. Everything got blurry. He looked at her white sneakers; they looked like fresh bags of ice. She had her feet neatly crossed. Above her feet, her baggy pink nurse's pants looked like an open wound. She once looked so fresh, so natural and beautiful. He could barely recognize her. Is this what time did? Make better soldiers outta everybody? The smell of metal and dry tin burning surrounded him. He began to feel panicked. Panic in his murdered, brittle heart. He began crying.

"Not anything! Not anything, you big lug!" She tisked as she smiled without condescension. "Oh, Duane! Don't cry, we'll go shopping! We'll get you a new outfit!" She laughed again. "Nothing always turns into something! Sooner or later, huh??"

Her lips seemed to curl into her tiny, fang like teeth. He thought, why was this mindless, bar bitch for Christ alive and his mother and sisters dead? He heard the earth crack like a giant bone. The apartment seemed to rattle. He felt smothered by her cheerful obsessions. Hazy confusion melted around him in the next couple of seconds. Outside the window, through the quick slashes of cheap mini-blinds, Mexican gardeners were planting a skeletal looking maple tree into a small brown hole.

"Oh, Duane! You've always been so sensitive!"

He began ripping at his ears as if his ears were the source of his pain. He fell outta his chair in one violent thud. He thought he passed out. Maybe he would dream.

Jennifer had left. She left the door open and he heard her large, new car speed out of the apartment complex parking lot. He stopped crying. His cheeks were hot and wet.

The door was still open. The sunshine was fresh and clean as it swept through the room with the smell of the freshly shoveled dirt. Dry earth. He walked over and stood in the brightened doorway. The bright, blinding monotony of the Florida sun flushed his face. The smell of dirt, strongly soured by the Florida air but healthy. The fresh air and sunlight were everywhere, ready to accept him, just as he was. He had his goodbyes. He had their power, boredom and cruelty. He had his own. And there, under the doorframe, he turned from human to mud to dirt but he felt humbled and strong as stone. And as stone he would finally be able to cry, cry and sing and sing.

That's what he's been up to lately, and now, that's all over, too.

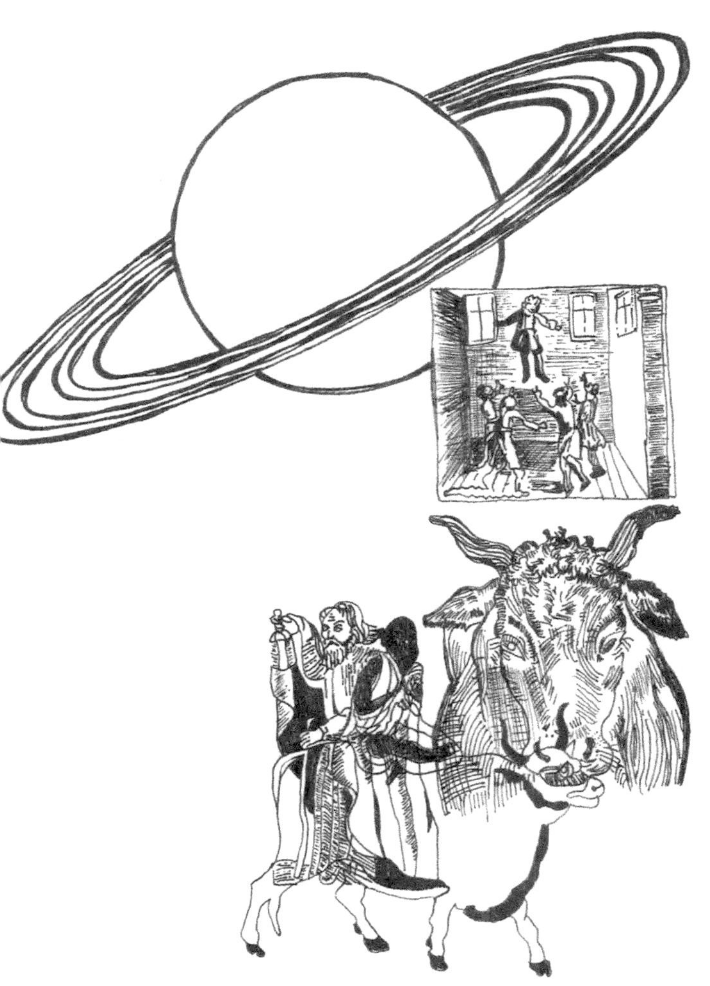

ONLY ELVIS REMAINS.

A manmade exorcism is taking place. The Hoover Dam has been demolished. Deep pools of murky water sunk the state formerly known as Nevada so far below land, beyond footsteps, strip clubs, bad diner food, boy's weekends and bright lights that there's no longer a difference between going to Nevada and going to the bottom of the ocean. Las Vegas has always been a lonely place, anybody sensitive will tell you. Now Las Vegas is abandoned in her wet grave. And who can say if she's lonely any longer? Days, days for normal American people, seem thinner and frayed without Nevada. Everything seems calmer, in a way, after the tsunami that took out the west coast left everything wet, drowned and destroyed.

At first, on the news, Las Vegas looked like a twinkling wad of Christmas lights in a murky kiddy pool. Throughout the rest of the country, people frantically bought Las Vegas postcards, t-shirts, snow globes and other traditional tourist memorabilia to preserve the memory of Vegas. But what does Vegas, let alone the memory of Vegas, matter now that it's gone?

The entrepreneurs hope to make a couple of bucks, for the future, and who can blame 'em? California is an island that nobody can get to and that seems to suit California. Why would progressive Californians wanna visit us in Unconscious Hickville, USA? Why would they wanna get in their new half-electric cars and drive outta their massive traffic jam?

Years have passed. Now, only Elvis impersonators travel from the disaster and back on the news. Years ago, when the exorcism happened, they strolled triumphantly from Vegas over to Utah. There's television footage of them doing just that about three years ago. Since the exorcism, the news plays the same footage year after year. Everybody is more truthful with what's really happening, even the news. That's why the news just repeats the same stories at different parts of the year, every year. Why report new disasters if underneath, the petty details of the disaster is really just the same old shit disaster to be told, to be feared. So, the same stories revolve around.

The impersonator story is my favorite story on the news, actually. Maybe because the news airs the story every spring, around Easter. The footage showed the impersonators walking with their dirty guts out as if they were following Moses to The Promised Land. When they got to Utah some two months later, they hijacked Brigham Young University and have raised every building on campus from potential drowning. We guess that's why they raised the buildings on concrete stilts but who the hell really knows what the motives of another people, let alone impersonators, really are?

In California, we hear that nobody can remember one Elvis song. It's like the flood took that away, too. The remembrance of good songs, that is. The flood took away the good songs. The water washed away all the original songs. They are forgotten but crap songs are intact for impersonators. Only the images of what has been remain.

Anyways, they're pretty damn good masons. I've done some masonry in my past and it's harder than it looks. At BYU, the impersonators sit Indian style on Persian Rugs, humming. Everybody is afraid of the ocean, of salt water and finally, of drowning. They think humming will float them. No instruments are necessary. No lifevests. Neither are words. The impersonators never take off their sunglasses or black wigs, and no cameras are let in now, so who knows what's really happening?

Who really knows what's going on in the present? Another year has gone by. Finally, something new on TV. Brigham Young University has been remodeled and renamed by the impersonators. It's simply known as The Mormon Wife Motel. The interior is a perfect replica of Graceland. Gold wallpaper surround men in tight, white spandex pants. White spandex pants surround tiny red and blue rhinestone embellishments. Bedizened rhinestone collars are tucked into course, dark sprouts of chest hair while the white spandex hides old, sagging skin, skin that hides hearts and beer bellies underneath, inside.

The Mormon wives have their own cooking show now, since they are world-renowned cooks. It airs every Tuesday night on the Food Network. I watched it yesterday and I tried to get my wife to watch too, so she could catch a lesson. At the end of the show, on gold baroque platters, perfectly roasted pheasant souvaroffs with goat cheese parisse and black mission figs were presented to a long table of jolly, red-cheeked and gin-blossomed impersonators in gold-rimmed sunglasses. The doe-eyed Mormon Wives smiled as they served in sensible canvas dresses.

Together, the Mormon wives looked like giant Ked brand sneaker, devoid of feminine sensuality or womanly mystique, but the meal was something to see! The sight of such a delicious, home-cooked meal glistening like fresh dew off of those gold platters sent shivers up my spine. Oh, it pained me, it looked so damned good! I've never eaten a meal like that. Just watching the comestible presentation made my stomach sing and my eyes water.

We watch. We can only stare at the food. The mainland is fed by the corporations. Food is cold in plastic, or tin or cardboard. Only the impersonators are allowed to get fat on real food. Everybody else has to get fat on fake food. It makes me sad to consider. With tears in my eyes, the impersonators raise their jeweled gold chalices to the camera and smile a drunk's oblivious smile to the camera. The American flag waves in the wind. An eagle screeches. The show is over. That's how it always ends.

Nobody can see the wind but it sure as hell can push things around. Nevada is gone. The deluge has broken. My wife would never wear a sensible canvas dress. She wouldn't want to roast a pheasant, anyways. Mainly she doesn't have a free moment, anyways. She's working or tending to the kids. If she does have a free moment, she flips through the tabloids that make her wonder about California.

Ah, California! We all stare at their adventures in magazines, that's all. Just stare. They have women there, in California, possessing a mythical beauty that no woman here could ever, ever have. Like the siren's song in Odysseus's melancholy journey home, California traps all the pretty girls in, as if they were flies or mosquitoes, and not the most beautiful girls with the softest skin and prettiest legs, asses and warmest breasts in this whole country. Insects. If you happen to have a pretty daughter or sister that isn't in California, she'll hear that song, that sonic vibration, California pumps throughout the country in magnetized beta waves, unintelligible to the rest of us regular peons, but not to the prettiest of all pretty girls in your hometown. She'll catch on and dream.

Dreams still carry us. Then she'll disappear, on a new moon night, the darkest of all nights, into California. You won't see her again. Who knows how she'll get there? She'll manage. And you know what? She'll be happier there with a richer, more luxurious life, so you'll be glad for her, in your true heart of hearts. You'll bet it won't be no time 'til you see her in the tabloids lounging on a beach in Hawaii!

Now an island of progressive consciousness, California is chalked full of golden sunshine and eternal youth. Sun and youth drives up and down highways in pale black automobiles with thick bulletproof glass windows. Inside their cars, they only listen to Red Hot Chili Peppers. The song "Californication" reverberates off of smooth Italian leather seats and hot, young asses but it's all inside, inside of course.

The state above Nevada is basically gone, too. The concept of a United States has gone with it. Dark, swollen water took everything that we advertised we loved away in a cold oceanic wetness. No more saving and dreaming for the long, boys weekend to Vegas. What happened in Vegas, sunk Vegas. Only bloated Elvis impersonators survived.

We live off of our memories. But that's a coast away, in the sinking state of Florida. That's where we live. The northern swamp, above Disneyworld and down below Georgia, where it's always humid, hot and senseless. I'm not an Elvis impersonator, so my kingdom isn't at The Mormon Wife Motel. My kingdom, if I had one, consists of seagulls flying like they are lost and crying through irrational orange heat, amusement parks once a month, and a salt-rimmed, monotonous humidity that warms your internal organs to a bloated foam in two seconds flat- but all that's on my days off. Those are my fun days.

The Everglades aren't California. Mainly I work. I'm at work. I've done the same work for twenty years now, during the day. At night, the twinkling stars press against the moaning sound of cold-blooded animals in a velvety, muddy darkness. As if this Florida shit makes the stars brighter, more brilliant here, and makes the rest of the world more horrific, more jejune, out there. Dead, brittle vines and teeming mosquitoes circle slime, garden statues and patio chairs alike.

Here the minutes turn into days. Years go by, another wedding, another bridal shower. Another beach picnic my wife attends in her happy neon print bikini top and matching, tribal sun-patterned sarong. Kids come, and kids go. Birthdays are all done with cheap rainbow-colored balloons, supermarket cakes and paper tablecloths. Another birthday. Time moves but it doesn't even turn up on the shore anymore. It shouts in increments like its lost. Sometimes time whines like the greedy gulls lost too far inland, and then hides, proud and bellicose in the Spanish moss and mud for a while.

Monotony is the only love that we know. Only hate, too. We stay inside the white paneling of our new starter houses, sun-tanned and swollen, while someone else has an air-conditioned Superbowl party, gets a rumored venereal disease, snot-green swamp awaiting, nipples hard and skin sweating in our beds, divorces and the freak accidents, another gathering with cinnamon scented candles in a jar, chips, chips n' dip, and chicken wings. Pizza Parties. Cheap walls outside, drowning inside, without gold wallpaper or Italian leather seats to remind you that you're important, too. You're a real somebody. You're a goddamned impersonator. You survived. Congratulations. Have another party. There, far away from here, you can try to impersonate life.

You can at least try. Tonight, I hung a new picture on the wall. It's an old west photo the family took at Six Flags, for fun. It's stained nicotine to make it look authentic like it's from the turn of the century. I hold a rifle. But I'm in the background. My sons, Timmy and Craig Jr., aged 10 and 8, hold bottles of Jim Beam. The boys don't smile because they're looking tough while my wife is tearing up the photograph with her toothy laugh. I can't hear it now, of course. I just stare at her face cocked back and looking up like she does when she laughs. Her high heel is on a prop-wooden table. She has a garter on. She couldn't stop itching it. Her thigh is a frontier, a moist, muscular cage, imprisoned by our two sons dressed like ancient cowboys. She wears fishnet hose, a soft pink feather sprouts from her skull. A jumping flame flashes off the glass holding our family's photograph in. I know she is standing behind me lighting a cigarette. I don't need to turn around to know she's there.

With all the impersonators in charge, it's easy to see that love is just another deformity. Something else to advertise. Nothing to get excited about. Nothing to hold on to with your egos. She's blowing smoke around my sweating back. But I'm moody.

I don't think I want much, but I suspect that I never got around to what I was looking to find. My big, hollow heart is broken, boiling blood. So, when it comes to what the water took away, or the manmade exorcism, I really can't say. I turn to her and tell her to quit it. She's always pushing my buttons. How many times do I hafta to tell that woman to not smoke in the house. To quit it!

She mimics me and says, "Quit it, quit it, quit it." Until

she's got a whole new song over it. "Quit it, quit it, quit it!"
    I'm fuming but she's the one who's smoking.
    That's how only Elvis remains.

HAPPY MARRIED COUPLE.

Until death do us part, my life will be busy and full as the husband in the Happy Married Couple. How long is life? I'm counting down the days. Until death do us part, we get to spend countless moments together. Doing household chores, working, taking care of the kids, eating. Sometimes, when we're alone and in the mood, we're allowed to be animals with each other. The rooster inside of me cockadiddle doin', the faux alligator skin panties she wears, meaning, in all these years together, she's ready to have a good time tonight! Heaven is an earthly delight in the middle of Florida. We live so close to Disneyworld but go to Six Flags instead. When mama's not happy ain't nobody happy. The ocean was warmer than your piss today. Every Sunday after church, 11:15, we all go to the beach as a family. We bring between seven and thirteen items. The kids swim and run around all day. At night, like tonight, the kids fall asleep wrapped in old comforters on the living room floor in front of the television.

The nightly news is on. A hurricane took out a whole trailer park in Alabama. This is given four minutes of airtime. Two teachers are making a difference in local high schools-two minutes of airtime. The mug shots of two seventeen-year-old black men are shown for twenty-eight seconds in front of a blue background with the stations logo in the right corner. Twenty-eight seconds, I count. I drink more of my beer. I don't want it to get warm. I hate that, warm beer. I've got thirteen minutes to drink it before it turns. I won't need that long. Tomorrow calls for some possible afternoon sleet, four seconds of airtime before the commercial break. Yesterday, I plugged up a hole in the wall that was caused by my frustrated seven-year-old boy and a Louisville Slugger. That took some time. The paint can is on the floor waiting for me. I watch the television, and the sleeping kids, in the mirror that says, Coors Light, in nice cursive. They sleep with their small mouths puckered and open. The blue and silver light bounces off the children's profiles, their opened mouths like blue fire.

Silver Bullet. I'm all suntanned, pink and drunk-swollen in the family photo, by the mirror. That was when the kids were smaller than her thigh, when they weren't so obnoxious and frustrated. When a cool breeze could make her nipples hard and chill her sweating skin to gooseflesh in less than ten seconds, but that was then.

That was then, when we weren't The Happy Married Couple. It was the past, where no house light shines, no paint can waiting on the living room floor next to sleeping children. Some things haven't changed. My wife likes three sweets at this time of the night: whip cream, Marciano cherries and good, cold, pink wine. Home is where the heart is in this over-ripe, sinking swamp. When she was pregnant she would crave Arby's. We would sit across from each other and each get the 5 roast beefs for 5 dollars, each. 10 roast beefs.

Missus and Mans, with matching brown curly fries. Those were the days! Ah, the days before I had the inclination of counting the seconds of airtime on the evening news. It was at Arby's actually that the counting started. Something out-of-grace happened to me 1,758 days ago at Arby's. Never been the same since. Like one of those movie narrators came to live in my head. Can't get so close to life, to living-no dat's not what I mean! Can't get close to the normal stuff of life, like watching the news, or shootin the shit with my co-workers, or fightin' with my wife, without this fucking voice of counting numbers, structure and time. The thing is, it's not really a voice but I just call it that because I don't know what the hell it is. It never actually 'talks'. It's subtler real-ly. It magnifies and clarifies the things that you see until it's brighter than tanning beds lights. When ain't nobody around, I'm fine! More than fine, I'm a juicy peach.

It was when the second son, Jack, was on the way. We went to Arby's to satisfy one of her cravings. It was August and my car's air-conditioner didn't work, and I warned her, yes

I did. I said, 'it don't work!' But she didn't care a squirt, so there. We cruised over to Arby's any damned ways. She complained that the air didn't work, even though I warned her. By the time we got to Arby's we were dilated sweat bags. Our skin was a salty rind of bloated toughness. I thought we were just going to keel over in complaints and heat exhaustion and find Until Death Do Us Part, right there in The Arby's parking lot, but no.

No. We slowly rolled out of the car and walked crankily together toward the doors. A polished, black Bentley was parked in one of the handicap spaces. The license plate demanded in authorized FL DMV capitals: GATR CTRY.

I knew that car. I knew that personalized plate. That was the boss's car. It was sunny and hot. The car sparkled like an exotic gun just left out for a child to play with. The sky seemed to shove its blue loneliness closer to us, closer to the melting black asphalt we walked across. I grabbed my wife's loaded waistline and pulled her closer to me as I hunched my shoulders down. I looked around for Big Man McNeal.

I didn't see him. Outside Arby's was Big Man McNeal's daughter and her friends. I suppose she was visiting from college. Strangely, they all had handmade signs on wooden signposts but I didn't see what it was all about because I was looking at McNeal's lovely daughter, wanting to make a good impression. What was her name?

She looked pretty and bored like the unplucked daisy under the lonely blue sky. She had big blue, almost purple eyes and long, straight blonde hair. Her tiny mouth sat like a candy heart in her perfectly carved, triangle-shaped face. I knew her since she was a baby. She went to Duke University now, I knew because Big Man McNeal never missed an opportunity to tell his workers how much her tuition cost at Duke University. Man, have I heard it, and done heard about it, again!

Reagan. That was it. Her name was Reagan McNeal, the boss's lovely daughter and the pride of Northern Florida. Out of nowhere, Reagan screams at my wife, who was nine months pregnant at the time, "Murderer! MURDERER!"

"What in God's name is she doing?" My wife responded to me.

"MURDERER!"

"MURDERER!"

"MURDERER!"

Reagan's face was a rigid red strain of screaming. Her friends all were screaming too. Screaming and jeering until they all looked possessed, their faces twisted with hatred.

"MURDERS!!!!I HOPE THAT YOU AND YOUR BABY DIE THE SAME WAY THAT THOSE ANIMALS HAVE DIED!!!"

When my wife heard that she began crying. She cried so hard that her belly heaved around like she was about the give birth. Soon every woman was wailing in some way or another.

"Now wait a goddamn minute Reagan!!" I screamed as one of the pretty girls lunged foreword toward my wife's stomach.

"Don't Reagan me you ignorant FAT SOW!!!" She sneered.

"FAT SOW!" Was repeated through the gaggle of girls as I swatted the pretty girl that was clawing at my wife. I pushed the girls away from my wife and into the glass and metal Arby's doors. A hand with a sapphire ring grabbed a chunk of my wife's hair and pulled. Quick like, I pried the hand away but couldn't get all my wife's hair outta her hand, then gave a strong push into the crowd, and jumped into the Arby's after my wife.

"Carnivores!" "Shit-eating CARNIVORES!!!" They scream.

They repeated that one over and over. The girl with the ring had a clump of my wife's course hair in her pink hand. She shook the hair around above her. It looked like a demented voodoo doll in a pink hot dog bun. Meanwhile, my wife's cheeks were red and swollen from crying.

The screaming over and over and over! My wife's dark hair

was sweaty and wet around her forehead and neck as blood came from the crown of her scalp. There was a missing tuft of hair. There was a hole in her scalp now. It looked like a repeatedly punched and busted up mouth. On her scalp was bloody gums, no teeth with her torn black course hair chaotically strewn about such red hell. I almost fainted. My wife kept crying like I've never seen.

My wife's tough, she never cries. It broke my heart to see her like this. She kept touching for her heart like she was making sure it was still there. The girls saw my wife crying and pretended to cry, mocking her, while yelling how cruel and dumb we were for being carnivores.

I had never heard that word before. Carnivore. Was it a cannibal? No. That wasn't it. Carnivore. It was a meal for an animal. A bloody food for animals higher up on the food chain. Afraid that my wife might give birth on the dirty tile in the local Arby's, I told my wife to breathe. The fat black girls behind the Arby's cash registers were the only real doctors to be found and I began to panic.

Holy hell did I panic! What was a man to do! This was the horror I've seen on TV and it was all happening, to me, now. Quickly, I grabbed my wife's head and began caressing it like it was a beloved basketball.

"WATER! WATER! SOMEBODY GET ME WATER…. AN' LOTS OF ICE!!!" I pressed her body closer to mine as I yelled again, "Somebody get my wife a water!" Her body convulsed hard but it didn't feel like contractions.

"You're okay, sweetpea, you're okay, you're okay…you're a tough girl, no need to get upset about that."

She cried harder. "My he-heee—my head!" She stammered through the tears. Her solid body convulsed roughly against my soft gut. The baby seemed to be punching her from the inside. Punching her repeatedly. I moved my arms down her back then softly moved them to where the baby was punching and yelled, "BREATHE! BREATHE!"

She wouldn't breathe. Her efforts turned into pregnant

woman's hiccups. I let go of my hold on her, lead her to a booth, and sat her down on the red vinyl seat. I looked at her soft brown eyes. I wouldn't stop looking at them. Same eyes she had before we were the happy married couple.

"You're okay. You gotta breathe though, sweetpea!"

She hiccupped some more and turned a ghastly color of old barbeque sauce.

"BREATHE, COME ON DAMNIT, BREATHE!!"

I fumbled in my pockets and shook out my flip phone to dial 911 but it was all good-praise the Lord, my wife began breathing again. And I began breathing. I let out a sigh of relief as one of the fat black girls behind the counter dropped off a XL cup of water and an XL cup of ice with a timid smile. Then, she sat down in the empty booth next to us.

She told us that the white girls had been at it all week. They'd be going back to school next month so she expected that it would last until then. We sat in silence while my wife drank the water. I applied the ice to her raw, hairless and bloody patch on her head and dabbed it with wet paper napkins. The girl who worked there didn't move away, she just looked over us and stared at the pretty and fired up sorority girls outside.

Their posters said, "Meat is Murder" and "You can judge a man's true character by the way he treats his fellow animals" and "Down with Carnivores!"

The Arby's girl didn't seem to be affected by any of it. She sat in her Arby's uniform like she had an even better uniform on underneath, and it wasn't made of cheap fabric. I don't know what it was, it was something I felt from her. I felt more peace than I had ever felt before. It was silent. The way silence can't help but to be unfathomable. The air conditioner was cold. I felt weird being so relaxed in the calm silence. Silence was always a torture to me, I liked the radio or TV on all the time.

I wondered if this girl dressed in an Arby's uniform was some prophet or a holy woman, at least to have such a peaceful presence in her silence. I felt like I was at one of those community plays where everyone's your neighbor, and a bad actor. It's real still and silent on stage and the lights get all harsh and dramatic and the actors are trying their best to be dramatic but hey, it's only your neighbor Bob Kirby in black pants and a black turtleneck. The drama seems ridiculous and then weird, dream-like weird because it's so bad. Sure, Bob is a bad actor but a great neighbor.

Even though the girls kept yelling at us with spittle and slanders coming from their mouths, I felt such peace. I felt like I had never worked a day in my life. The peace of nine hours of sleep, or the peace of being at the ocean all damned hot-week. I felt that silence. It was beyond all the noise. It was the silence for all.

My wife had closed her eyes. A silence for those with no way out, no fine ideas, or God, or talent or smarts to go on ahead, and raise 'em up to sit fine like a princess on Daddy's lap for a long while, a long, long while, too. It was a silence for pigs. For those who eat pigs. A silence for carnivores.

Reagan commanded me to leave the Arby's if I was half a man. I watched her yelling but I was a million miles away, here, but in that silence for carnivores. That's when the voice, or light or darkness whatever it was, came for the first time. Soon, Reagan with her Bentley and fine education seemed desperate, so full of rules, conclusions and finally, so full of hate that it made her a puppet. My wife seemed confused like she dozed off and had woken up and didn't know what was happening. I tried to explain that we were bad people for eating mistreated roast beef. She shook her head and winced. She stopped shaking her head.

Reagan beat at the window.

I yelled, "We just eatin what we can afford!"

I have what I've always had: the cheap stuff, whether it's the silence, insults or the mistreated roast beef. But what does my dumb words matter? This tiny, passing life circumstances that I relate to day after day? That I think is me. Eventually the smart girls left and then, we did too.

I started seeing things differently. I don't know what to do. I drink too much now. This I will admit. The voice, that's not really a voice, done came in my head. There's a distance to everything I see, like everyone is performing dumbshit community plays. Nobody knows that it's just some bad show because they get so wrapped up in the performance. In the feelings and judgements, bound up in suffering and reasons to hate, and being so smart and cocky about hating.

The voice won't hush. It never says anything specifically. It just shifts my perspective until I see more, until I see what's underneath. Maybe I can hear thoughts. It's very quiet. Grocery shopping becomes a nightmare. Everybody's a psychic Kathy Chatty just blah, blah, blahing all over the frozen food aisle and I'm the only one who can hear it. Nothing is quite like they're telling you it is. I've gotten so withdrawn, my wife even made me have a talk with our preacher after Jack was born. When I done told the preacher about the things I had seen and heard from the narrator in my head, he just smiled at me like he's paid n' made in the shade. He breathes like he's breathing in the sweet, sweet golden air around the baby Jesus.

I even tell him about the bad community play we all are living in. I leave nothing unturned, as this man is the professed vicar of God, no matter what bozo sideshow I sense in him. I say everything, and I mean everything. He just kicks back like he a man who got shit figured out. Nothings a big swing. He exhales so deep that I swear I smell the son of God born in a manager.

He bellows, as he is fond of doing when he got the Lord in him, "The wisdom of this world is folly with God!"

"Fine. That all sounds fine enough." I say. "But what's that got to do with me? I'm a bulldozer operator."

Ah, those were the days, though. 5 for $5 value meals. Those couple of hours where we were stuck in the Arby's, without our 5 roast beef sandwiches with the angry rich girls outside. 5 for $5 value meals. Now the prices have doubled. Now there are three kids, Jeff, Jack and a new baby girl, Dorothy. Like I said, we live so close to Disneyworld but go to Six Flags on the discounted days instead, maybe three times a year. Nothing too deep in life or in dreams, the smell of an exposed sump pump in the summer heat, and the kids grow up singing like a chorus, "More! More! More!"

More cheap meat sandwiches. Man, this is the life. This is my world right here. I said that with a beer in hand on the beach this afternoon. Tomorrow morning I'll be gone from the beach, gone to work and I'll be another man among men in hard hats, t-shirts and work jeans. Just standin around with hands on our hips showing protruding bellies. Our chins pointed to earth, each T-shirt a different color of neon.

On the back of our shirts:

McNeal.

Simmons.

Horton.

Griffens.

The names of contractors, and their men, tearing the Florida swampland down to earthy muck, leveling all vertical, sylvan nature to mud, worthless sticks, cutting the life of trees and deep green plants into a muddy death stew ready for concrete.

It's horizontal living. Who's going to live on this tortured, mangled land? And what dreams will dream these people dream in their new starter home on this mangled land? Do these people even dream anymore?

We'd never have the choice to live like this. I drive forty-five minutes to work every day. We've moved three times, each time more inland, since Jack's been born. We can barely afford our rent. And you know what? Small fries. Small fucking fries. Sitting on that bulldozer with a hangover from hell, I'm popping Tums like sick candies.

It's all small fries and Tums. The weekend came and almost went. This morning after church, on the beach, did you see how I looked at you? I love you as I know the silence loves your body, your every confused thought so efficiently, so gently that it loves you with its presence and not with its memories and dutiful gossip.

I love even your fight-that fight you got in you, girl! How I found new depths in my love for you. The seagulls swarm over us letting out shrill yells, fighting over a Dorito the kids dropped in the sand. I'm dumbfounded by this love. The baby's pink sleeping face under your sweating bronze breast, her red exposed face, waking to cry, the heart-wrenching newborns cry, confused, blurred deep eyes barely with pupil. The seagulls move in closer with sharp orange beaks. The kids are screaming and running, throwing doritos in the air and laughing. You were sweating and pissed as you said, "Are you ever gonna fucking help me?!"

I just shake my head. I'm a goddamn mess, girl. I gave you my world, but you were too slow to read it, and quickly I skulked away. Later that night, in the privacy of our own home, I spanked your ass with the faux-alligator thong on each numerously dimpled cheek. That thong looked like a muzzle. I crow like a rooster but you tell me the lil' uns asleep. I take one more swig of beer before I lay down. I'm asleep almost instantly. Doritos, Dorito. I don't count, I see Doritos everywhere. The silence takes it all away. The more fucked up I get, the more I know that the silence loves me, and again, I turn into a small chip, dusted in preserved synthetic cheese, for the creatures of the air to nibble at, tear me up n' enjoy. Then forget that I ever existed.

A GREAT EVENING FOR SOFT-BUTTERED ROLLS.

A great flood is taking place.

The Hoover Dam is demolished. The state formerly known as Nevada sinks under pools of murky water. Nobody was too upset about it. The major news syndicates never had so many viewers tune in to their 24-hour, live coverage. People are making money. The right people are making money.

Something else happened: days grow quicker, skinnier, and frayed as flotsam the flood carries away. Nobody notices that time has sped up since the flood. Now years go by, another wedding, another bridal shower, another daughter dressed in all white ready to be christened in the faith of your choice, fast and clean, squeaky clean, with corporate advertisements in-between until she's dressed in white again on her wedding day. All done up with cheap balloons in pink and blue, another baby's birthday.

And then another, the next day.

And then another, a couple of hours after that.

And then another, until the whole neighborhood seems like fucking junkies on speed pushing their grocery store carts with cheap grocery store cakes inside for another fix, another celebration, rushing for that feeling, free of pain. It's another party. It's going by so fast. Who thinks about stopping anymore? Who thinks about resting? Go, go, go! Fucking go. Go, eh?

We're moving here. We're full of so much anxiety you can't really tell the difference between coming and going, between being happy and being driven by fear. The years move, but they don't turn anymore, nor do they linger, they keep going quicker, unearthly fast but it's all inside. Inside the white paneling of their new, more and more, fucking NEW! starter houses. New and more new.

Believing in our circumstances, whether good or bad, has

turned us into junkies. Our entertainments, loves and wars are immediate. In New York City, the sophisticates gobble up renovated brownstones like they were Betty Crocker brownies. More people are making money. Others are left like fucking junkies celebrating another birthday. They move to the country. Somebody else has a Superbowl Party, goes to the prom, gets a venereal disease and meets their first grandchild, all that same night. Divorces and the freak accidents carom together through weddings and 4th of Julys like oversized cymbals, the metallic shivering sound, over and over again, through every human's nervous system. We all sense this speed. Another gathering happens, and people start to panic because earthly time is moving so incredibly fast now. The life expectancy lowers quickly. Nobody makes it past 60. What the fuck is the sun doing moving around this earth like a dunked b'ball? WTF. That is evident.

There's nothing else to fear. The end is near. The news ratings take a dive. People lose money. The right people lose lots of money. We all know what's happening, there's no need to watch the news and mull over it. No need to become sticks in the mud. The real junkies pushing grocery carts are in a vengeance glee and celebrate another fucking birthday with rare American gusto. Oh! It's evident that something great is happening. It's so simple and true. It's like sunshine reflecting on the ocean.

You like that TV? It's dust. You like that chair? It's dust. You like your body? It's flames. You dislike your neighbor's personality? She's gone. It's all done, baby. The running sun drools off its edges like ejaculated orange sperm and there, there, underneath all the slime, reveals a heart. We were all very surprised. It's in a sky every color of the rainbow. There's no need for anything superfluous like fear, anxiety, buying shit or fear, anxiety, selling shit on our devices.

We feel something we've never felt before. It's more efficient than we were ever taught efficiency could look like. A coast away, the state of Florida is sinking. Everyone was evacuated safely and effectively. At Disneyworld, Cinderella's Castle sticks out of the swamp like a decomposing claw from a drowned, mean cat. The time that usually separates this event from our life from that event is gone. The breakneck pace, obsessed with arriving, and Go, Go, Go! moves on. Wildfires. Who can survive the bad brightness of our Brand New glow? The radio stations can.

"Go! Go! Go!" The songs on the radio sing. The songs on the radio tell us who we are.

Around here, nobody can remember any song unless the radio plays it. Nobody can. Not the television anchorwoman or gas station clerks or the shop girls at Dillard's. That's where the Radio Kings come in. Sometimes they play Elvis. When they feel really lost, they play Elvis. They help us to remember The King, if they feel so inclined. The King is a memory. No more kings. Memphis is gone. Now Florida is gone, too. The concept of a United States is also gone. Only radio music happens.

Radio music and little, twinkling lights in dark swollen water where there used to be restaurants, nightclubs with bad heartbeat music and hotels and "Fun! Fun! Fun!" remain. Now "Fun, Fun, Fun!" songs have turned into "Go, go, go!" songs.

Both Elvis and the lost world of pace, of waiting without celebrations or devises and boredom is lost. Human patterns exist on the surface, but for their existence on deeper terrain they need the plasticity of the brain, your brain. Until the pattern is implemented, it remains scrambled.

Did you know our brains are the consistency of warm butter? So, break out the dinner rolls. Civilizations teem with sidestepping maniacs that nobody calls maniacs, but successful people who keep a breakneck pace in their mania for spending, saving and possession. Spending replaces Democracy. Press repeat. Play it on the radio. Labyrinthine structures demand laws, that I know.

Christ. I had to tell it, again. I had to tell you about The

Great Flood, again. You know why? Well, lemme speak plain to you: What I couldn't see took me a long time to get over, and what I did see wasn't enough.

MOVING.

I'm in my green velvet and white fur trimmed dressing gown and stand at the window watching the plants press their fragile bodies on the glass. The air is wet and minerally on this fresh, early spring morning in the Pacific Northwest. The lush plants outside wave around in the short gusts of wind and dull fog. I study the green colors outside for my newest watercolor painting. My house looks like a seashell, or an ancient political arena in a giant green sock. In the wind, thick emerald ferns clash against jade leaves of plumeria pushed over the eucalyptus trees toward our windows. The fog made me wonder if I was dreaming or sleeping. If I could package these colors it would be easy, but I have to study them, know them until I possess them, to mix the perfect hue.

Everything seemed to jump out at me, and purr with a life tougher than the life that coursed through my thin veins and pulsed, evenly, through my artistic heart. The Pacific Northwest?! What sort of life is this? How did we wind up here?! It's too good not to be true.

I wonder about it. I wonder what sort of food makes the massive tree's roots sinuously and thick, but I have no answers. I don't need answers. I don't know what sort of ingenious soil makes the trees so tall. I have plenty of time to wonder about trees. I have plenty of wealth to wonder about the meaning of food. Food, nourishment. But you don't have to say everything or say yes to everybody. You don't have to give all the time. I jot some notes down in my diary about the relationship between color and humidity and notice that the kids have left. Billy and Sarah's car is in the shop. They took Hank's car to school today, and soon, I will take Hank to work.

We have just moved here, to beautiful Clackamas county, Oregon from Washington, D.C.. We are very excited that our dear Hank has been newly elected as the Surgeon General of

Oregon. Our house is really our dream house and everything is just so wonderful, peaceful and so sure, that I feel happy, beyond happy. We've unpacked most of the boxes ourselves, that is, the new maid and I, and we only have a few boxes in the dining room left.

I'm waiting for the newly hired maid to come back to unpack the rest of the house. We must give her something to do, you know. Yesterday was her first day and I don't like to think that we're paying for somebody to sit around all day. That's basically all she did, yesterday.

She's a short, squat woman around 35 or maybe 65, it's hard to tell with Mexicans. She perspires from her forehead, says okay miss too much for comfort and smells like a warm comforting soup you would give a child with the flu. She seemed sleepy, thirsty and hungry all at the same time. She came in breathing so heavily and complaining about her allergies and missing the bus and walking here with her dingy plastic grocery bags full of cleaning supplies that I had to stop listening to her. Well, I was tolerant, of course.

She seemed to not be able to catch her breath the whole day. When I did give her a chance to sit she acted like she was going to faint. Oh, everything has just been so lovely, lovely, lovely! I can't let the maid's laziness get to me. I'm only troubled by mother, but these things have a way of solving themselves and I don't need to worry unnecessarily.

I can't save Mother. My new therapist is just fantastic for telling me this. It was so simple and yet I had missed it for so many years! Now every time I want to extend some kindness to mother I stop and think of my therapist's words, I can't save Mother.

And it's true. My kindness was disempowering Mother. I need to be more rational. Mother finally moved out of the Florida swamp (where Hank and I met at medical school) and moved to California in the progressive city of San Francisco. Mother is shorter than me with a thinner bone structure and tiny heart shaped face with big blue eyes. Eyes that instantly make you feel love and peace when you look into them. She smells like sumptuous silk lingerie that has been closed in a cedar case for too many years. She's so delicate that she seems like a ghost, sometimes. She looks too long out the window and when she walks she seems to float right above the floor. Certain people were suspicious of her in San Francisco. Certain people. They treated her differently she told me, and I told her not to be silly. Who would treat her differently? Mother feels as if the old successful hippies of the Bay Area are only performing kindness or compassion or whatever those sorts of people find worthwhile in life. She thinks they're phony bologna.

I'm much stronger than mother. She just is a bit socially awkward from living in Florida for so long. She was strange to the old hippies because what old woman would drive across the country, in her new silver convertible Mercedes Benz (that we bought her as a pre-birthday present) and decides to move into a tiny shithole apartment in some god-forsaken barrio in San Francisco, and change her whole life around? To what purposes?

She was running, they thought, running from something, running away, and it didn't matter how liberal this retired, academic landlady proclaimed that she was, she eyed my mother in the most unacademic and thirsty way, like a coyote eying an abandoned chicken. Well, she didn't want mom to rent her apartment.

I witnessed it myself. It was about two months ago that I met Mother in downtown San Francisco to look for apartments. She found one in a disgusting barrio among run down bars and restaurants. Instead of a garden lining this sick brown building there was a slew of dumpsters and loquacious homeless people.

I didn't know why Mother would want to move here and strangely enough the landlady was giving Mother a hard time about renting. It didn't matter that Mom had a perfect credit score. This woman thought that mom was 'a criminal running from her family, running from the law, running from the queer, lowly state of Florida. A hillbilly. Yuck'. That's what she told Mom, in French.

Mother doesn't understand French but she does understand hostile emotion and the woman had enough of it. The landlady wore a green velvet jumpsuit that was so clean I began to frantically inspect it for one piece of lint, or perhaps a tear, or a drip of this morning's breakfast. There were no imperfections. A green Monet print silk scarf was tightly tied around her neck. On her little feet were soft white booties with white mink interior that seemed to grab and cling to the green velvet hem. She looked successful and clean through all the muck around. It is difficult to be an ambitious woman in this world, I knew the frustration that comes from too much clarity. The landlady was a former French teacher at Berkeley and insisted on speaking in French. It seemed severe, almost deranged, to speak in a romance language with not one speck of dust on your clothes but I knew it was tough to be an intelligent woman in this benighted society. When Mom told her she didn't speak French, the old lady pulled at her graying widow's peak and then began rambling, in French, about the heartlessness of people, the stupidity of American people, while tying her Monet print silk scarf tighter at her neck. Mom obliged her by looking down, like a shamed little girl as the woman begrudgingly hissed her assaults in English. Outside, a homeless man began screaming The Star-Spangled Banner.

I had to step in. For Pete's sake, it took me about an hour of discussing Marguerite Duras's Malady of Death, in French, to cozen this Francophile into renting to Mother. The barrio was very desirable for 'thinking, young, designers' the French twat hissed at me. Mother was neither young or a thinker and she didn't want her around. I told her there was an unpopulated barrio without desire, here, available to all women, of all ages, on this shitty earth, in French. The pining Francophile ate that one up. She loved it! The sounds of garbage trucks picking up metal dumpsters and vomiting their loud contents into metal walls. In the end, she rented to Mother with rare gusto and invited us to her house in Mill Valley sometime for petite pastries.

But the intellectual French twat was right about a lot of things. Mom was running. Mom was really running from her crappy southern life, her dead third husband, who was found dead inside his mistress's house, inside her shower and then, inside his mistress, who lived some four houses away, and Mother didn't know what to do, so she moved, so what's so bad about that?

Upstairs, I hear my loving husband, Hank, Mr. Hanky Panky Himself (haha!), walking around, getting ready for work. The heater kicks in as I stare at our ivory marble dining table. It seems to bleed against the eggshell colored wall.

The phone rings and I take my time answering it. Looking over the work that the maid did yesterday, taking a quick inventory of her sloppy efforts, egregious scrubbing skills and perhaps lack of commitment, I dedicate myself to future clemency with her lazy ass. It's alright, I think. I am the bigger lady here. I won't yell at her. I will correct her.

"Hello."

There's just a muffled sound.

"Yes. Hello. Grimley residence."

The sound of an old woman's sobs. It's a horrible sound.

My heart overcompensates by an upward rushing sound of my own blood. Blood rising towards my ears. Like a reverse waterfall of blood. The sobs continue until I feel soaked in my own blood. I've never felt so awake! Soon the sobs catacomb with my blood and it feels like a corset around my ribs and soft stomach, being pulled and tied, tighter and tighter. I get dizzy and lose my balance. It's Mother. I gasp for breath as if breathing air could help me find the floor. Mom's crying again. She cries because she thinks life is hard, brutal and shocking, soft as battery acid on hard, stale bread. You could break your teeth. You eat it. Hard. You ingest your poison.

You eat it, anyways. There's no barriers between you and life when you're all alone, and I wouldn't know. What exactly is life? I can't imagine. I have Hank and the kids. I feel as if I am going to have one of my fainting bouts. Would it be terribly bad if Mother came to live with us for a while? Then I think of my therapist. How Mother makes most sense when I am talking about her to my therapist. She cries to feel better. I give her permission. I do not have to take care of her.

"Oh dear, what can the matter be!" I gasp through the sound of my own blood swirling unevenly around my head.

"Mom! Mom! What is it?!" I try to breathe. "Mommy??"

Nothing except muffled cries and heavy breathing.

"Oh dear! What can the matter be!"

But all I hear is her muffled voice and frantic breathing in the phone receiver. Then the sound muffles. I know that she has placed the receiver up to her neck. She does that a lot. She puts the phone down to daydream out the window. Even when she's panicked and sad. I know her neck is warm, maybe even sweating. I remember her smell. Like something mysterious, unconquered, feminine. The way that she smelled when I was a little girl, when I was frightened about something and I would hug her and grab her neck. I was afraid of unreasonable things as a girl. I would clasp her neck and she, in return, held me so close to that warm, soft-scented body. I could smell her warm, flowerly-fleshy smell. I felt how much I loved her and she loved me. Is this what the tiny birds around the deep green robes of St. Francis felt? I moved toward a wall to balance myself out. Spins.

"Dear! What's the use in all this, huh?"

Nothing was said. I got irritated.

"Stop this at once!!" I replied to my inquiry. "Stop this infantile nonsense, AT ONCE!!"

I suppose freedom has a time limit.

Therefore, it's not freedom.

Nothing, no one, no one replied.

"Mom? Mom?"

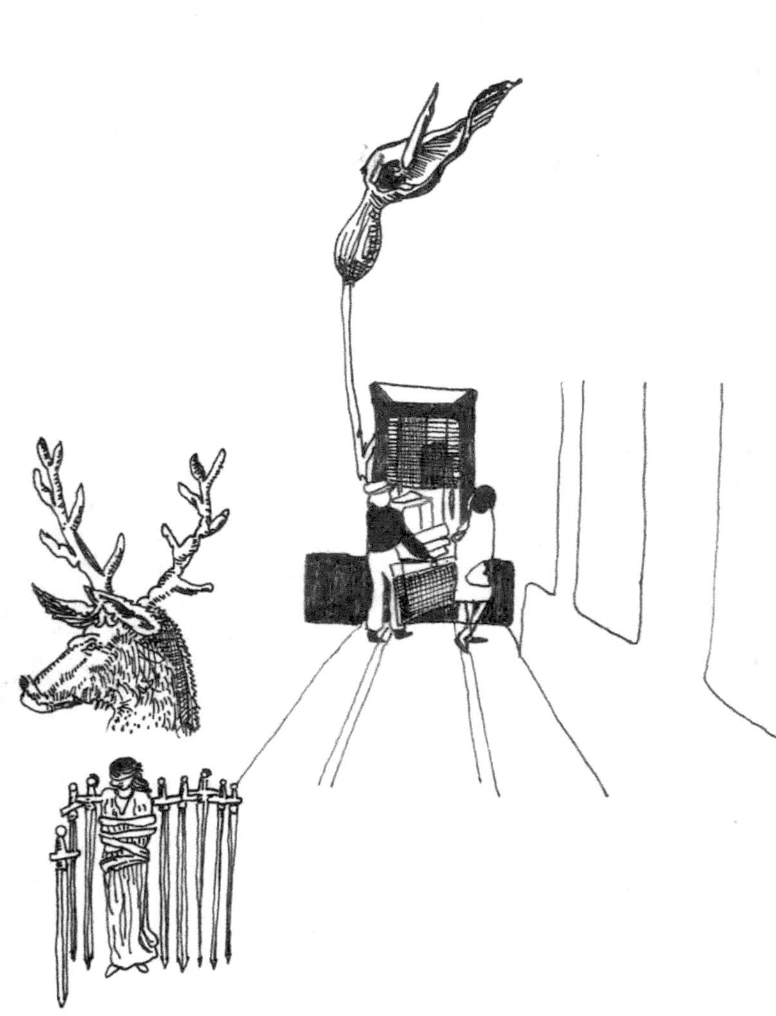

But she could not stop crying.

"Mommy?" Crying into the phone again, because she left everyone and now she knows it for sure. Because she is old, everyone has left her. She's never been alone. Mom's lonely and had lost all this weight to prove it, and my sisters are punishing her now by not answering her calls, by pretending that she never existed. Beyond the ivory dining set and eggshell white wall is a large breakfast window. Outside the window, an expanse of grass, the shape of a fetus, I now notice, and a freshly planted citrus tree. Beyond that, the old, unplanned trees, tall and thick, look menacing and wild in a creepy sunshine that beamed through misty air; like light and smoke from a film movie in an old, defunct movie house. I hear glass bottles breaking into a dumpster somewhere and her muffled cries.

"Oh dear! But what can be the use in all this!"

The maid has left herself in. I hear her locking the door behind her.

"Mrs. Grimley?" She is walking closer to me.

"Mrs. Grimley? Good Morning?" She says more timidly as she sees my face.

I look at the stack of boxes through the sound of Mother's crying and heavy breathing. I feel paralyzed as I sneer at the new maid. She is rather discourteous by making me feel uncomfortable and confused, in my own home. I want to scream at her but I'll wait. I will make her feel worthless and humiliate her, in my home, after I deal with Mother. There are all sorts of ways to keep things orderly. All sorts of ways we keep matters in boxes. To live inside the narcotic, starved effect of boxes and use our lifeblood to live in straight, unfeeling and rigid lines. I know why heart attacks are on the rise. It's all ways that we keep ourselves from truly caring for our loved ones.

I shove these thoughts away. But every minute that passes I felt as though something was wrong, terribly wrong. Alone, waiting and aloof, close and distant, trees everywhere around me while Mother is alone, in a big unfamiliar city, panicked.

I won't cry over it. The fog already weeps. Mother must be reasonable! She can't keep running away. Escaping is no good.

Can she stop her heart from beating so viciously? Can *anybody*?

The white furniture in the white house says nothing.

Let's move on. Would you get it if I stopped here or should I repeat the beginning at the end, for good measure?

Should I tell you what my outfit looks like again?

OH! DUMB, LONELY AND SAD HEART! SHUT IN SKIN AND HAIR AND TEETH.

A field. Affluent suburb of New York City. Over green grass laid thick, high-quality blankets. Blankets made for the rich by untortured American girls from good enough families with good enough credit scores. Children and teenagers sat with their moms and dads on these blankets. It was Saturday afternoon in Greenwich, Connecticut, sunny and springtime. The young Judy Garland should have been there with the entire Meet Me in St. Louis cast!

Mother and father robins sang over their nests in newly budded dogwood trees. Pie-eyed brothers, sisters and perfect strangers alike sing, sing, like they were all in a musical from the good ole days of the USA. What were they singing? It was better not to get sucked into all that. Some normal people held hands as they danced in happy circles.

The newspapers reported that kidnapping was on the rise. So were school shootings and the debt of a typical household. The newspapers made it seem like we all were being carried away. Nobody was going anywhere though, not literally. I looked around. Things happen in other ways. I looked around. It was a typical summer Saturday for my family. There are other, more efficient, less dreary, and psychologically meaningful, ways to abduct the innocent.

I adjusted my tortoise shell glasses as I thought this. I don't like glasses with frames, I never have, especially tortoise shell. They're uncomfortable and slip around easy which causes me irritation. My wife bought these for me because she thought I looked better than I usually do with them on. I look sexy and like I know what I am talking about, so she says, I look even sexier. The turtle shell bothers me. A tortoise shell frame thickly outlines everything I see. It drives me ½ way insane, honestly. I keep them on because I realize that my wife is the one who has to look at me though. If she likes what she sees, even better.

I sat on a newly bought, warm Pendleton blanket reading a book by Joseph Conrad while the whole rich, white town were having lots of fun. Our child and our baby were asleep next to my beautiful, smart and talented wife. A wisp of her blonde hair fell into her face as she read an article in The New Yorker. She didn't see me admiring her and soon, I looked down at my book. I began reading again, and soon, I didn't notice anything going on around me. I'm not sure how much time had passed.

I read in the sunshine. A passage took me by so much alarm that I stopped reading and threw the book down furiously into the grass, not on the new blanket. My wife giggled at me. I watched our neighbors begin to round up people off the blankets to form teams for a tug-o-war game.

"Oh, must you always carry on like that?!" My wife mentioned jokingly. "You're so childish!"

I didn't reply. Then, I picked up the book, cleared my throat, and reread the passage that made me furious out loud:

Few men realize that their life, the very essence of their character, their capabilities and their audacities, are only the expression of their belief in the safety of their surroundings. Their courage, their composure, the confidence, the emotions and principles, every great and every insignificant thought belongs to the crowd. To the crowd that believes blindly in the irresistible force of its institutions and morals, the power of its police and of its opinions.

My neighbors laughed and screamed as the tug-o-war game began. I'm surprised they weren't playing golf today. They love golf. They are forever playing golf.

Soon, one team toppled over. A fat man named Bob Kipling, who was the CEO of some national home décor store, was at the base of the rope. Quickly, he was pulled through the new grass and tore a patch of grass to pliant mud around him. There were more laughs. I looked at the patch of grass with the muddy roots like it was a green hair pulled from a brown scalp. Bob was filthy as he got up. People laughed some more. His red, white and blue Tommy Todder outfit was ruined. It was all in good-boring, non-humor-pawned-off-as-humor fun. The understated stuff of friendships for the affluent and the respectable. Why did they equally laugh at lame shit and at really mortifying things in others but if their hairdresser made one wrong snip they'd act like they were crucified?

Yes, others. Yes…to the crowd. I knew that we were well off at someone else's expense. Our laws and economy, our entertainments and games were set up like this. I didn't think to absolve myself or deny it. My wife was the daughter of Tommie Todder, the famous New England clothiers, for the love of God. I knew that this picnic could resemble a scene from Meet Me in St. Louis because somewhere else there was no picnic. There was no young, pre-boozed Judy Garland singing her abused heart out. No Old Hollywood. No somewhere over the rainbow unless you were fortunate enough to die. There was no golf. There was a rocky, drought-ridden terrain, so dry that there was no need for a sewer, populated with dirty, hungry people with guns, no dentists and mouths half full with rotten decaying teeth, the other half with emptiness and the voracious human capacity for craving, craving to fill holes. Certainly, there was no public water system somewhere away from here.

There was violence. Excrement in the streets, brutality and no grocery stores to sell you bloodless, corporate deli meats, or pert bank tellers named Jessica or Allison with meek tech school smiles and vixen coos, welcoming your avid business at your local bank. No newspapers to tell you about massacres when the massacre was all around you. Desert dirty. No wireless connection. Uneducated, no water.

I watched my neighbor's sons and daughters scanning their newest iPhones as their parents stood in semi-circles laughing, drinking high-gravity beers in bottles and chatting. Each picnic was so perfect that it looked like it was competing with the next. Most picnics even had their own floral bouquets in ceramic vases of water on little metal or wood tables or linen tablecloths. Another tug-o-war game began. Jovial competitive screaming ensued. More tugging between two sides. Soon every smile coming from the whole cast of Meet Me in St. Louis seemed like a deluded, arrogant vanity.

Why play tug-o-war? Why bother? Why don't we all sit around, get some harp players over here, and get fucked up while listening to at least forty harps, or take a big snooze? That seems really special. To listen to 40 harps outside, in nature, with your family and trees alike and dream? Who were we to read The New Yorker and sit on delectable blankets? We don't wield heavy artillery that chatoyantly dashes like stabs of white light, in the gory bagginess of the desert sun as we travelled on donkeys or outdated dirt bikes. Our skin is supple not salty, or beyond salt, leathery and tough, from travelling to one gravel ridden grave to another, never hoping for anything more than water. We knew the sweetness of stringed music. We want more than water and stale bread. We had drive. We had our corporate radio. We had our devices while others had nothing to drive them to live another day except that hidden, massive and illogical urge the body has towards brute survival.

While we are outwardly civilized, say we are non-violent and respectable, we are also inwardly fixated by the proper and consensus psychopathic obsessions that are all over the media, until we're all cruising on cruise control prescription drugs with our non-bloody concepts and respectable delusions. At least these dirty desert people appropriately call their war with the apt title, 'war'. We called our war peace. Are our articles about human life and 'the world' more precious to us than human life or 'the world'? There were no minorities here. We made it seem like we were part of The Meet Me In St. Louis cast.

I never asked for such thoughts but it's true, the summer is here again and I can't stop what blooms and I fucking hate Tommie Todder. I got up from the blanket and walked pass the many picnics, passed the fun, and more fun, towards the woods. At the manicured hedge of the woods was so much litter that I grimaced. It looked like an overturned trashcan. Stepping over a curb of litter into the woods, the temperature changed. It became chillier and I walked more slowly under a deep canopy of shadows made by old oak trees. I shivered as I walked on further. The soft earth was the color of seaweed. It smelled like musty bark. The silence was thick, guttural and soft as the earth. I walked further. Time passed. I jumped over a small, gurgling creek.

I walked slower and breathed deeper. My breath seemed to come from the soles of my feet instead of my nose. I became lightheaded. The sinewy trees with their course of hectic branches above me mimicked my own veins, and I felt at home. The woods were the emerald, pine green and kelp colors of the sea. Here was something that I could reach and not only reach or see- but fucking touch, without trying or competing for it. I couldn't reach many things in my life. It's true. I couldn't reach the park even though my family and I sat there every Saturday. I couldn't reach my wife and when I did touch her, I wasn't really there. I couldn't even reach my own mother. She didn't know why I left Florida. Why I married a woman like my wife. Mother says that my wife is more of a man than I am. I have no connection to the picnics except anxiety. No connection to women unless I let them be the man and turn myself into a woman. No connection to the land or to the manicured nature choked with fertilizer and properly suffocated until all her best, most inauthentic and ghastly bright colors expelled out in her stalks, blades and leaves.

I walked further thinking that I'd never go back to the picnic field again. When I got some miles in the woods, a little girl was sitting on a large boulder. She was alone. I stopped behind a tree to look at her. There was nobody else around. Her lanky legs looked sharp and thin, like eagle's legs on the boulder and she sat like she had been there for a while. She had dirty brown hair in a snarled page boy's haircut.

She had on drab wool blanket the color of dark mucus. With her subfuscous threads, she looked like a decrepit priest in a church's Nativity play, and I found this adorable. It reminded me of my rotten childhood outside of Tallahassee, Florida. I had to wear an outfit like that every year. My mother was proud that I was cast as Joseph, Joseph again. Pine cones were on the ground around her and she had a pine cone in her small hand and turned it slowly while she watched it. Oddly, she had fresh pink fingernail polish on. I stepped out from behind the tree. She turned to me and looked at me rather incuriously. She didn't say anything. I was offended. Why wasn't she afraid of me? Why was I afraid of her? Looking straight at me she said in a faint voice, "Oh! Dumb, lonely sad heart! Shut in skin and hair and teeth!"

She had cat-like green eyes and stared at me with the same persistence as a cat stare. I felt dumb.

"Who me?" I said. My voice travelled across the rocks and tree branches.

She didn't do anything except stare at me with her wild eyes.

"Who me? Are you talking to me?" I repeated.

She poised herself to jump down off of the boulder but waited and sat poised like that, like she was going to pounce, in the shadows of the tree branches above us. Further off, in an almost indigo sky, wispy clouds costively dawdled across the sun.

"You live in a sad inverted night." She said.

Probably, I thought, but didn't answer.

"Now, you'll see the daylight. So, why don't you just scram?" She said even more cuttingly. Next to the boulder, crows roosted on the pine tree branches, their heads tucked into their breasts. Further up were birch trees shading us from the reappeared sun.

"Scram? Where did you learn such an archaic word?" I laughed. "How bizarre! What a bizarre child!" I laughed hectically. "You sound like a Hollywood mobster, eh? What a riot!" She didn't move. Maybe she disappeared. Maybe the crows took her away. Maybe she turned into a crow or an eagle. I couldn't say. Strange shit. I walked back to the picnics.

Soon, I jumped over the hedge of litter and walked through the warm, green lawn as two boys yell over a Frisbee. A little girl in blue gingham grabbed another little girl's long blonde hair and pulled. Girlish wails. Another girl dropped her phone onto the sidewalk around the park as her friends screamed their laughter at the cracked, broken screen. A father runs, yelling at the boys who are now fighting over a Frisbee.

By the time I got back to the blanket I had changed drastically. It happened so quickly and unexpectedly, I felt dizzy. I was saying to myself words, words I would never choose to say in a voice that wasn't mine but the little girl's voice from the woods. She repeated over and over in my mind, "Oh, world! Full of broken hearts, conclusions, births and inclusions!"

I sat down and surveyed what was going on. People sat on their blankets. The picnic looked and felt staged by the graphic design that money makes. Some sat at picnic tables with red and white-checkered tablecloths, pushing away the gnats from melting ice cream and their baby's chubby face. The day is getting warmer. I put my hanky to my son's mouth. The nanny moves away. My wife takes her last swig of chocolate stout beer from a brown bottle. I notice that I can't see my tortoise shell frames. My heart leaps as I touch my face and realize that I don't have my glasses on.

I'm dumbfounded when I realize that I can see perfectly fine, better than fine, I can see oil pooling in each and every one of my wife's pores. I look to my children. I can see spittle, copulating with spittle from each taste bud in our baby's mouth. I shutter. I see how many worlds are available in this bland one.

I open my leather satchel looking for the glasses. Nothing. Worse, dust mites and fomite. I frantically tuck the book into a pouch with folded newspapers in it. My wife didn't notice me trembling. She had something to tell me about a brilliant article she read in The New Yorker.

Oh, how I wanted to close my eyes and grab her by the wrists and shake her and shake her until the rigorously maintained flowering kale and daffodils shook in their designated flower area of the park. How I wanted to scream, 'But The New Yorker has nothing to do with goddamned life! It has nothing to do with the slow, steady sucking in and wheezing out, and in, like a rabid dog, and out, in and out of the ribs of vast, inexplicable living! How wild the days really are!!!'

But my wife was very excited about it, and I'm no poet. All around me nice enough people were very happy that it was the weekend. Could it be that I had better than perfect sight? What should I do now? What was one to do but watch the grass grow until you can hear it rise from the soil out into the air, changing color every couple of seconds in its newborn bloom, only to get trampled on by all those ugly monotone shoes who house people who are mean in business and super-amicable personally?

Maybe I was having an LSD flashback. I got further in. How can you read The New Yorker, anymore when you realize that they only publish the accomplishments, lifestyle statements and perspectives of the appointed serious people? How many articles, let alone serious news venues are really just another one-dimensional queue of neurotic, bland citizens who adore the possessions of others? Then arrogantly fight in the battle to distinguish themselves from the mass of men. The picnic and the fertilized Peter Pan green grass seemed like a poor excuse for life from beggars, affluent beggars.

Poverty comes from the illusion that pretends. I looked around the picnic. Everyone seemed so clean and detached, like they didn't even need the sky above us. They were poor people, the rich. It's sad to see people for what they project themselves knowing that they're not that, at all. It's even sadder to see people as they really are.

My wife was still talking. She's great at in-depth analysis of her favorite articles. Not only will she read an article and include her opinion, she will tell you about the research the author included in the article to prove his or her point. Then she will tell you the various contrary research that the author chose to elide, and if the author obfuscated any of the facts or not. She is very keen. She has had a lifetime of leisure time. Her knowledge is a sport. She wins, she likes to win. She kept talking and I was nodding my head at the properly appointed times. My children were playing on the iPad. The nanny was pretending to watch them.

I spasmed. She didn't stop talking. I spasmed again, in shock. I couldn't see the tortoise shell frames to my glasses! Quickly, I moved my hands to my face, again. I could see that my wife's face was in a foul, dirty smog. Then, as my wife spoke, something strange happened. The destitute little girl from the woods was in front of me, reaching out her hand to shake mine from the middle of my wife's oily, porcelain forehead.

It was the wrist and little hand with fresh pink nail polish coming out of my wife's forehead. But as the hand birthed above my wife's familiar eyes I realized it wasn't the destitute little girl's pretty, delicate hand at all. It turned into a large, calloused hand of man who had died long ago from some war-torn country that no longer existed. The resilient hand that knew the outdoors, extended toward me. And as that rude hand shook mine tightly, I knew the whole underground world in one lonesome and strange handshake.

When I returned from this dream, something even stranger happened. The dream didn't end. My wife had disappeared. So did my children. My whole rich Connecticut town disappeared. The litter disintegrated and turned to autumn leaves. I disappeared. We all disappeared. Our homes became outdated and vanished. Our careers were gone, too. Pinecones scattered the lonely places we once knew so well. Our CEO's and their families moved to what was formerly known as Lebanon. They formed a community like Greenwich there. They still play 18 holes of golf on green grass. At night, they trade defunct baseball cards over expensive bottles of bourbon. Every day they drive their golf carts over the rocky dirt to the mall and trade poncy socks before they play golf. They have survived and brought their way of life with them. But who do they have to talk to? What do they really hear? They're the only ones that are left. How very little they really have. Only the pinecones and daffodils hemming in the green field where we once picnicked are still there. They turned red as blood. Crows cawed to one another as they crisscrossed the deep blue sky.

How odd, odd to want to continue playing golf so much that you let everyone suffer and die around you and then instead of helping them out, you walk over them, and ignore them. You ignore them so well that you whistle while you leave this country and waltz over the ocean with your Callaway golf bag over your shoulder like Santa Claus carrying a bag full of toys. You'll continue golfing. You golf in your new homeland and instead of ignoring the people you used to, you ignore the natives there, wanting only to continue playing golf, not carrying about men screaming or machine guns firing, or even living, as much as you care about playing golf…and then?

ROBBIE KIPLINGS'S MANDATORY ESSAY ON THE PREFRONTAL CORTEX: MIN-PONY UTERUS, HOTROD, CRASH

(OR, PUNISHMENT SCHOOL WORK: AN EYE FOR AN EYE REALLY DOES MAKE THE WHOLE WORLD BLIND BEFORE YOU CAN DRIVE!)

The first blizzard in twelve years blows outside my window. All I can see is white. All I hear is the wind but the snow is so dense that it looks like nothing is moving. I shiver at the sound even though I'm not cold. I sit at my desk in my bedroom. I like being alone in the house. My parents are in Hawaii for their anniversary. There's no school today but I am suspended, anyways. I like knowing that even though I am suspended from school, all my friends aren't at school either because of all the snow. I like the snow so much that I don't mind writing an essay on 'Independence'. It's funny to be punished by institutional public education with 'Independence'. My hero, Miyamoto Mushashi said, 'Perceive that which cannot be seen with the eye.'

Independence exists in the prefrontal lobe of the brain. That's what scientists say. Nobody really cares what the prefrontal lobe looks like even though it holds something so royal, heroic and dignified as Independence. I looked up images of the prefrontal cortex online. When I saw it, I knew exactly what it looked like. The prefrontal lobe resembles a min-pony uterus.

You know what springs forth from uteruses? Babies. Newborns. You know what babies get into? Anything. Everything.

The prefrontal cortex must resemble an animal uterus. Everything trending and inspired nowadays comes from the prefrontal lobe. All 'higher' consciousness, 'higher' intelligence and personality comes from the prefrontal lobe. It's a very high place for looking like a tiny horse uterus.

The truth is that I really want to become a samurai. That's what got all this crap started. My samurai schtick has gotten me a lot of hell, actually. So much so that I'm suspended from school for mouthing off, and on my forced vacation.

I'm going to graduate high school in two years and already people want to know what I am going to do, and where I am going to go to school to do it. They want me to pick an occupation that matches my intelligence quota. They wouldn't bother me to fit in so much if I had a normal IQ but since I 'show genius' they want me to be like them, but better. That way they can be proud of me. I don't want to be like them. Especially better versions of them.

I want to be a samurai. That's it. They say to join the marines. They even sent some turd from West Point to come talk to me. These people obviously don't know what a warrior, or war, really is. I feel sorry for them, really. I feel sorry the way that most people make themselves so puny, confused and easily duped. Samurais aren't like that. Samurais are warriors, they don't live in cataloged concepts, and even more, compartmentalized distinctions.

Independence as well as all rote systematic functions of society, like social control or obeying institutional authority comes from the same part of the brain as Independence. This makes me aware that Independence is jacked from the get. The special or bland way of responding to that authority, deciding and acting upon what's right, what's wrong, and regulating behavior goes on in a part of the brain that resembles a horse uterus.

Planning, cognitive behavior, personality expression, aesthetic visual perception, policing, decision-making and the moderating of appropriate jokes/ levels of inebriation/ response-reaction-all happen in the prefrontal cortex. Conceptually, the prefrontal cortex is a strange house party at some guy's house that nobody really knows, but it's definite that his parents aren't home because every high schooler, low life and sketchball in town is there. They even say this in the typical, boring and fiducial way on Wikipedia. This area of the brain holds everything.

People tell me that they are concerned about my fanaticism with samurais. They say that someone with my IQ shouldn't be concerned with irrelevant old ways of life. They say that no one would take me seriously as a samurai. That hurts my feelings. When I tell them to fuck off, I get suspended from school for a day or so. Applicable linguistics and apt semiotics, just good, wholesome planning, like having a college education is what matters for them. All of this is born in the prefrontal cortex.

Being born to a min-pony or a human is a matter of mammalian eggs and doctor snipped bellybuttons. It is a matter of having a prefrontal cortex or not. Once you have a prefrontal cortex you have an identity, you live in society. Uteruses are not like the prefrontal cortex. A uterus doesn't have to know consciously what it's doing and a perfect, adorable baby or baby pony comes out for the whole world to love. Birth among farm animals is really exquisite, even celestial, if you get into it, and it's no surprise that in Christian soteriology the Son of God was born among such beasts and stinking fodder.

With such esoteric and earthbound changes, it's easy to see that nature is forever changing, even in the dense physical world of beasts of burden, high school and mud. With such transmogrification nothing is really as it seems. Not even here. Here, in a land of Independence, Opportunity and Free Thinking where some are born into managers and some are born into mansions.

In the USA, Independence is important. It takes an animal uterus to be born on land as an animal. Independence begins inside a woman. We have a day dedicated to its namesake, in the hottest month of all, July. On Independence Day, the adults get publicly drunk, and the teenagers get privately drunk, and together we light fireworks into the dark sky.

During the day, we grill cheap meats on the bbq and shove it between white buns made from genetically modified wheat, at corporate factories and eat them with our families, neighbors and friends.

In The USA at sixteen, we get a little snack cake of Independence, and we can apply for a driver's license. We don't learn how to ride a pony. We don't have ponies on the freeways, anymore. Most of us don't own horses, a horse is not a symbol of independence anymore although it once was. We are not Cowboys and Indians. We are law-abiding citizens. A car is a symbol of Independence.

Independence is connected with movement, going places. We use our achievements as fancy cars, also. With our achievements we cruise up and down nighttime streets skirted with the people that we care about impressing, while they, in turn, look bored and don't notice us. We drive on. We want to be popular and noticed.

Most car crashes are by teenagers. Kids don't know what to do with the sophisticated motor equipment but who can blame 'em? We're all learning, right? Crashes happen every day. If you get in a nasty crash and you're a popular American, like James Dean, and you die, you're instantaneously reborn by another great American Uterus called The New York Times. Another transmogrification.

You'll be on TV, too. Dead men, soon to be dead, are all over the TV.

There's an alternative to this macabre rebel gruesomeness, though. It's called living with the proper social controls. Being a good kid. Being a good kid is signaled from the prefrontal cortex, also. If you lived on without crashes, graduated from high school, then graduated from college, and did all the normal, not too dark stuff, like worked for at least twenty-five years at the local Bank of America sector by the Village Cinema in your town square, you'd never be front page of the newspaper. Never. Doing the ordinary things doesn't grant you professed Independence, fun holidays, or celebrity.

On the radio the song says, 'Only the Good Die Young'. The people driving in their cars and listening to the radio live on. They sing the song without actually wanting to die young, or perhaps really wanting to be good, for that matter. We can't all just drop like flies! We want other things, too. We want to live the good life.

To have the correct conditioning, to recognize when someone does a 'good job', to obey an outside authority although any authority or independence or adherence to doing something well comes from the inside in an area of the brain that resembles a horse uterus, well, it sounds like poop to me. I wonder and I wonder many things that aren't very esteemed to consider. I don't deny it. I'll probably be kicked out of school for good when they read this.

What if there was more to it all than the abstractions that we make teenagers write about? What if there was something else besides the concepts that justify war? What if we could see 'reality' as something else besides social norms? To live inside this Uterus we are all in, anyways.

What could happen? Would we all hug trees and ban GMO foods? Would we all quit our jobs, play ring around the rosy in big green fields, and be quite happy about it? Would we all watch the same captivating TV show at the network's designated hour slot for our entertainment?!

Would we still differentiate among conflicting thoughts?! Would we do heinous things like take our neighbor's wives, join riots in grocery store parking lots, break the windows from Radio Shack and Restoration Hardware, alike? Steal all merchandise? Would we need a means to get to the ends anymore? Would we need time, at all? Are causes for effects a horizontal process? A blizzard to blur the lines of a day like today. Just to wonder about it all.

The prefrontal lobe of the brain, without social restraints and dense, very polite and wimpy ways of social etiquette, class warfare, war and sex and drugs and prescription drugs and conditioning? What is it really? The wizardry of using shit, and I mean shit, like a samurai? To see the punishments as rewards and rewards as punishments. To drive beyond all punishment and reward.

The laws of isolation holds true. God, let me find out if it really is as dark, dark and big out there as the honorable men have said before me.

CHIMP AT A TYPEWRITER.

William 'The Bone Cage' Matthews is a five-year-old chimp who has lived in captivity at the Lincoln Park Zoo, in Chicago, Illinois. He has never been outside his caged area of about 29 feet by 14 feet. William has never felt the earth under his toes. Can you imagine? His world consists of concrete.

Concrete floors, concrete rewards of Pavlovian bananas, when he's a good monkey, janitors with steel pooper scoopers, industrial size brooms and buckets of diluted bleach that scrub off the residue of William's shit every morning. People who look like janitors portioning out meals in the morning, midday and night and the occasional scientists and rich donors to the zoo smiling, smiling nervously, as they unpeel another banana and bend down to hand it to him. Take a picture. Smiling. Substantial things. That's nice. That's life!

In the cold, concrete corner, The Bone Cage sleeps in fresh hay. A child's desk with a typewriter and a child's chair are his possessions. There, in his cell, good scientists do experiments on The Bone Cage. Nothing inhumane.

The scientists want to get to the bottom of things. Specifically, what is the distinction between human belief versus animal conviction? William, the chimp, is there to enlighten them.

Today, an incredibly cold Tuesday, after a random blizzard at the end of March and news that a man killed 479 people at a football game, The Bone Cage sits at a typewriter and types: qwwwwwwwwiirrrmnnmnyynynynynynynynfkfkfiiafnafksxxxits peaceful on the mountaintopSofofofofofofofoooooooooggn-ngnksgkgsjhfsghsfdlghisltrt

Inside, behind glass, scientists sit and stare. They are in starched, bleached coats with their doctoral surnames embroidered in blue over their hearts. On their computers, they record the new data. Its peaceful on the mountaintop. Some of the scientists wear fashionable eye wear. At the zoo, man and man's predecessor, the chimp, sit. They either sit inside, or outside the glass, in the cold damp Chicago afternoon. They are observed or observing.

It's peaceful on the mountaintop.

There are many things that we don't understand but that's because we're like chimps.

But Aw God what does it mean!

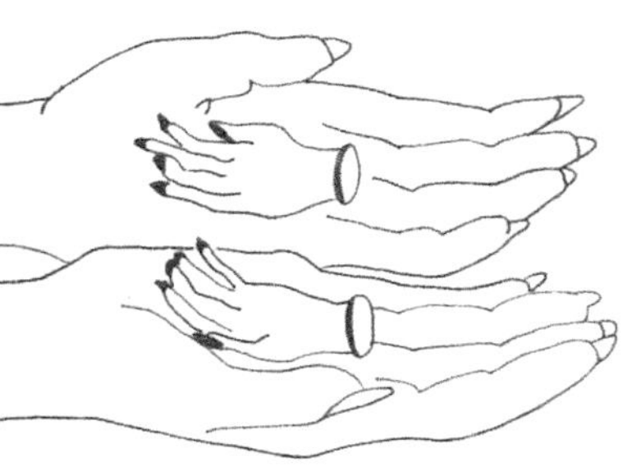

ANOTHER STORY ABOUT THE PRE-FRONTAL CORTEX AND DANIELLE STEEL.

(THE TREES HAVE BEEN REMOVED FROM THE LAND OF NOD)

Pretend that you're looking at an average map of the brain. In front there's the prefrontal cortex. In the prefrontal cortex there's an area, anterior cingulate, which is known as the 'striving' area. To strive is to wear a collar and be strapped, jerked and choked at the fancy of the leash and the anterior cingulate is appropriately collar shaped.

People who lack stimulation, or, who have massive brain injuries in this part of the brain report a feeling of rejoicing and ultimate contentment. I'm one of the trauma patients here at the hospital. From our trauma, ecstasy made it's manic and grandiose home in our damaged brains.

Our mirth tickled us absolutely pink! Every day was pure revelation. We didn't need to go anywhere to get excited. We didn't need to make plans to look forward to vacation. We didn't need to think positive thoughts. We didn't have to visualize the things we didn't have but wanted to have.

'I just didn't wanna. Didn't wanna at'll!' Some patients would laugh when asked why they didn't move all day.

We wore adult diapers. It wasn't so bad for us. Like being drunk and pissing as you swim in a lukewarm pool, kinda cute feeling. Honestly, it felt like heaven. Happy, happiness colorful and engrossing, cheer that didn't worry if I was brain-dead or going to be a vegetable my whole life and then worse than dead, a burden to my family. I genuinely smiled for the first time in my life and it was like a great generosity. Happy. Happiness all around you, whatever was around you, couldn't help but to ripen, turn a couple of shades brighter, or darker, and bloom inside this heavenly perception. One day I spent nine hours looking at a rubber tree plant and I felt bliss knowing that this green creature had pores and ears and a voice. How could we not be devoted to the subtle? Top neurologists gathered us here to live in a laboratory, in a hospital, to study us, three hours north of Miami, Florida.

I had been here around seven months, they tell me. Most traumas resulted from large objects bludgeoning the patient's heads. But the trauma was a blessing. How grit that irritates the oyster becomes the pearl! From this phenomenon, the neurologists called the anterior cingulate, 'Mixed Blessing' after a novel from the writer Danielle Steel. The brain trauma patients, like me, who were sedulously studied, were called Danielle Steel and then a number.

We met in the morning for weak coffee and grocery store bought cakes with the neurologists and their secretaries. Neat rows of yellow pound cake diagonaled moist crumb cakes with chunky crumbs, dry croissants sat in the background as those artificially colored rainbow cookies were tossed in the front.

The smell of antiseptic, urine and wafts of weak coffee in the cold, white room with an even colder, more impersonal tile floor held us. I remember the backaches from too many nights in hospital beds. The stiff personalities from the neurologists. Our family members coming during visitor's hours only to cry all over us, our trauma, rabid memory loss, and our soul's psychic leaking, all blossoming under harsh, almost dyspeptic, fluorescent lights. But what did It matter? I had paradise.

It was our trauma-induced revelry that caused us to rise above petty human views about such n' such. It was our trauma that revealed the multifarious umbilical cords that deadlocked us to mystery, all of life and harmonies. It was never broken, no matter what they say. We were the lucky ones. We sensed how great it was to be human. We felt better off than angels.

Sometimes various holy men from their respective religions were there as experts decided if our 'New American Samadhi' as they wrote about in Time magazine, was, in fact, actual Samadhi. We drank coffee in small, manic sips like we were Willy Wonka incarnate and every day, every day, we were genuinely surprised. Some of us couldn't even help but to cry a little in joy and appreciation over the mass-produced, corporate morning cakes.

We were mandatorily obliged to talk about our condition while the neurologist's secretaries recorded our talk for the mornings. It wasn't so bad. We didn't mind much with all the bliss everywhere.

Today Danielle Steel #11 started things off by dramatically declaring, "The trees have been removed in the land of nod. It's the perfect temperature outside…" he stopped and picked lint off of the right shoulder of his hospital gown, "yeah… around 70 degrees. But no trees. Nope, no trees. Green lizards…"

Danielle Steel #6 cut in, "It doesn't matter if you start flying! Hey, Jim, I didn't know your hat was made from a goldfish bowl!!!"

Danielle Steel #11 finished by saying, "There's no this, then that in the land of nod, Doc. There's no trees, see. Whatta you know with all these damned lizards!" He ended with a wild expression of happiness on his face.

"And there's ripe peaches scattered all through the grass here," another one of us pitched in. "Plucked from the invisible branches. Each peach is perfect, beautiful, not an inch rotten, discolored or saggy. My God! Just one bite! Just bite into one and know real salvation. If everyone could feel weather this good! It's just so delicious right now."

Danielle Steel #23 was not fond of coffee. He drank that crappy Lipton's tea shit in those cute paper packets. But man, could he put down the pastries! He didn't care for croissants or bagels- he preferred pastries with enough icing on them to look like they'd been dipped and dried in vats of sperm. And he devoured them like crazy. He usually ate enough to make the nurses come in and hide the pastries with icing from him but today was different. He didn't need the sweet treats.

He said he already ate. He said he wasn't hungry. The neurologists perked up. When asked what he ate he told us he had roasted peacock spiced with only the morning dew of wild gardenias. The gardenias had to be wild, he specified. The scientist's secretaries recorded this, as #23 shuttered in presence. His belly bulged. He shoved his hands between his legs by his knees and looked about. Maybe he did eat a peacock.

#5 was staring at #23. They began a staring contest that lasted some tense five minutes. Nobody said anything. Peacocks flew everywhere but the sane and those in a contest didn't notice. Maybe I was the only one to see these peacocks. Finally, they both laughed, together, like little girls.

"It's blue, ohhh exquisite blue, everywhere, doc!" Danielle Steel #5 excitedly relayed from his laughs. #5 had been a construction worker his whole life in a rural town outside of Allentown, PA. He was a bald, heavy, an older man with an undefined face that would be easy to pass over except for his swollen purple-red drinkers nose. Quite a honker splashed with tiny red veins. The red veins seem to crawl frantically from his nose to his two droopy ears, as if there was solace in his ears.

"The kinda blue the sky is on the first warm days of spring." He said like he was in a Broadway show and about to bust the place up in the first song.

"The blues that make you stop." He paused and put out his hands and shook them. "Stop! Stop! Stop!" He bellowed joyously.

"And maybe lie down, forget about work! Remove your shoes and socks, and melt into the soft, new grass sprouts around you. Ah, that calm blue where everything on earth is young, fresh and growing around ya." He laughed.

"Like your stuck in a thick…what's it called….a thick… oh, yeah…..those Easter eggs…yeah, Cadbury crème egg.

Every day is fucking Easter! You don't need a calendar to tell you. Ah, it's too good! Just swimmin' in it!" He crossed his arms over his potbelly like he just told a great joke while the rest of the patients all laugh with too much abandon.

The staff looks annoyed as they usually do. Danielle Steel #5 waits for us to stop laughing but he knows he's gonna have to wait a while. We're all laughing so hard! And he begins saying, "Well….Welll…..Welll….."as he cracks up too.

After ten minutes, nobody is laughing. It's quiet. We all smile like children. We are pleasantly exhausted. Danielle Steel #5 goes on, "But I know that this isn't what really happening, of course. I'm not in an egg at all. It's not Easter. It's never Easter for me. I'm not in a park at all. I'm in front of you in this cold room…" He looked down at his shoes.

"…and, an'…I don't know what you've done with my shoelaces…and…an' it doesn't matter! I feel so good! Sooo alive!" He nodded eagerly. There was a pause as the doctors realized that that tears flushed over #5's face. Their secretaries began typing again.

"As if the whole world caught on fire and the flames didn't hurt nobody because the flames were the…um…jewels…in emeralds, topaz, rubies and amethyst. Like everything was made of jewels!"

"Like a whole world in which pain had never even knocked on the damned door. Like there ain't no doors...no doorknobs." Danielle Steel #12 slowly spoke as he slowly rolled his neck. Then our morning talk was over.

The neurologists got up and looked at us all like lunatic bums, breathed heavily, and quickly walked out. We sat around.

The neurologists enjoyed playing golf on their long weekends. We thought playing golf was stupid. We didn't need activities. It was learned that most of the patients were from the working class, and most lived below the poverty line but, here, we didn't care about making something of ourselves to get outta it. Here, nobody gave a shit about winning the lotto. Nobody wanted to win. Nobody wanted to go anywhere. These cold hospital rooms where we lived were just as well as the Four Seasons Hotel. Going nowhere and taking no pictures while there was the most honorable thing about being alive.

The trees have been removed in the land of nod, it's the perfect temperature outside. All activities are asinine. And they are.

You know what it's like here? Heaven. So fuck 'em. Ripe peaches scatter about the green lawn under an exquisite blue sky. Nobody else is around, and you're not waiting for a damned bus or a soul, either. You're not waiting for nothing to happen. Your life isn't hinged to something like that anymore.

Something happened to us trauma patients besides being hit in the head with a large, hard object. It's sorta Greek now that I think about it. The Greeks didn't slice their blessings from their curses. They understood that you can't separate these things.

They gave me an operation two weeks and seventy-four hours ago to correct the brain damage. My head is shaved and my gaunt body looks like a plucked and dehydrated chicken. I've not seen the sun and been doped up on prescription drugs for so long. I was the first Danielle Steel to go through the procedure successfully. They have a dumb version of success though and give me a week to live. They are a poor people, the doctors.

They gave me a week to live. They gave me an operation that took away my peace. They are poor people like that. They cut every goddamn thing down to size. Even my life. Sure, I understand about the doctors. It's a way to see. To see like everyone else.

All they care about is studying your diseases. It's not their fault, their knowing comes from deduction and exclusion. Always looking on the outside for a reason, and once they got it they slice n' dice all n' sundry until they got a machine outta the whole mysterious universe that makes sense, that's easy to use. For them easy, easy for them to use. You wish you could help them but they're the ones who are supposed to be helping you out.

Worst of all is that I have lost my bliss. I had something really special, you know. I never knew love like that. Now in my bliss hangover I notice that people who are besotted with names like happiness, individuality, or success often don't have what that name signifies in their life. So, they get obsessed with finding it. We spend our whole lives like this. We're taught to go out and get what we don't have. In this sick theory, only the miserable pine away for happiness and romance, only the discriminated care about justice, and only the very poor care for wealth. The ones that are on top use the insecurities and weaknesses of those on the bottom to become more rich, happy enough and call it success while the ones on the bottom believe them. But what sort of dumbshit success and happiness is this? I wonder.

We force our great, misguided ideas into reality and then call them facts. If that wasn't ambitious enough, we drag them into our everyday business. But a funny thing happens when our bright ideas, our happy names, become mostly divorced from the very idea that they say that they were in the first place. You see how poor the rich really are. How sad the happy are. How happy the sad are. I became weary of the ways people control one another. I didn't need to leave the hospital. I knew what it was to live. It turns out that the whole world is really upside down. It's certainly a Mixed Blessing.

They feed me anti-nausea medication through an IV. They feed me opiates through an IV. Anything in or out is through IVs. Now that I'm normal and not elated, I know I'll die. I'll blow this popsicle stand. Then I'll return. I'll reincarnate. I'll come back and wear a white coat. I'll label the whole world with my coat on, and I'll have achievement stacked on top of awards. Then I'll die again, this time after what they call a good life. Diapasoning throngs of celestial votaries engulf me. I join them. You should hear our rebellious, dithyrambic songs. The Siddhis say I got here through the good acts of my past karma. There's peaches everywhere in the land of nod, like one of the patients said but not one damned tree.

I smile expectantly and act like I don't know much as my relatives pour over me, crying, crying and pinching the thin flesh on my face as I try to move away from them, but they can't understand. I can't understand. I do try to understand. It makes me uneasy to see all the people I've ever loved stand in these cold, sanitized 'guest' rooms and cry as they surround me. Cry like they know something that I don't. I feel nauseated, like my bony body is a small make-shift boat, half destroyed and mangled plywood. But it's being carried. Floating now further, now faster and faster, along some dark, dark and demented river where the water is blacker than the night.

I'm getting smaller. I'm so tiny to this dark river that it carries me along faster. So tiny that I don't have the energy to really look around me anymore. I huddle up, holding my limbs and head in a ball, I feel like I'm moving so fast. Then my family leaves. Designated visiting hours are over. I feel so shaky alone now. I miss them all. The echoes of their familiar tears baptize me into death and dread and the seedier side of life that my little mind, my littler words cannot understand. Can't do anything to help.

Maybe this is what happiness is all along. It has little to do with me. What I think of it all. I remember their faces and the echoes of their voices in the darkness.

Although there are peaches everywhere, really delicious to eat, you'd think I'd be wrecked about not seeing trees anywhere.

THE END

DANIELLE STEEL

MAN BURMASTER